# Wyldblood

## Issue 15 — Spring 2024




**Wyldblood Magazine #15 - Spring 2024**

© 2024 Wyldblood Press and contributors.
Print ISBN-978-1-914417-19-1

**Publisher:** Wyldblood Press, Thicket View, Bakers Lane, Maidenhead SL6 6PX UK. www.wyldblood.com **Editor:** Mark Bilsborough. **Fiction editor** Sandra Baker. **Subscriptions:** 6 issues epub/mobi/pdf delivered to your inbox £20. 6 issue print subscriptions £35. Single issues available worldwide via Amazon and from wyldblood.com/shop

**Submissions:** we are regularly open for submissions of flash fiction, short stories and novels – check our website for our current status and requirements. We are a paying market. We also need artwork, people to review us, and people to review *for* us. Email contact@wyldblood.com

**Issue 16 will be published in September 2024**

# Editorial

*Mark Bilsborough*

Ah, it's been a while. Those of you who've been with us for a long time will have noticed that we've slowed down of late, mainly because of other, pressing, demands on our time, which has distracted us more than I would have liked. But that hasn't stopped us packing issue 15 with some great stories from all over the world, from writers old and new. This time around we've got new things from Tiffani Angus, David McGillveray, Jessica George, Michael Teasdale, Chris Cornetto and many more running the gamut from hard science fiction to soft, wistful fantasy with races, robots and all manner of strangeness to keep you entertained.

We'll speed up when we can, which will be later this year. We intend to publish Issue 16 in September (though, in fairness, we intended to publish Issue 15 in March and it's now April - sorry) and then kick off with more regular issues in 2025. We also hope to have two or three novellas out in the Autumn and we'll be continuing with our fortnightly free Flash on the website – we're hoping to have a hold-in-your-hands print collection before too long, too – we've published over 175 fine tales so far and the best ones deserve to move out of the aether and onto your bookshelves.

So we're still here, still dedicated to unearthing great science fiction and fantasy and letting it loose on the world and still full of big plans and daring schemes. Stay with use while we continue to catch our breath.

A few things have happened in the Speculative world since we last met –

we've lost authors Christopher Priest, Brian Stableford and Vernor Vinge, amongst others. Priest was the acclaimed author of novels such as the Prestige (World Fantasy Award winner) and won the BSFA novel award four times (*Inverted World, The Extremes, The Separation* and *The Islanders*. He was married to author Nina Allan. Stableford wrote over 70 novels such as *The Empire of* Fear and *Halcyon Drift*, but more significantly for us, his 1979 novel *Wildeblood's Empire* bears an uncanny resemblance to the title of this very magazine. Coincidence? Maybe. Vernor Vinge is perhaps less well known in the UK but that didn't stop him racking up five Hugo awards and popularising the concept of cyberspace.

Speaking of awards, in the UK Eastercon has come and gone, and that means the British Science Fiction Awards. Juliet McKenna was the well-deserved winner of the novel award this year with *The Green Man's Quarry* (we'll review it next issue), but fittingly amongst the other awards (for longer non-fiction) Chris Priest's widow Nina Allan picked up an award. He'd have been proud,

Oh, and we're on Bluesky now (@wyldblood.bsky.social), which seems to be just like Twitter used to be and not like X has become with all of its intolerant nastiness, so come on over and say hello.

Enjoy the stories.

# Winter Wears No Crown
### *J.L. George*

"Truly, Mersa, this isn't necessary." Rhin spoke through gritted teeth, the muscles of her shoulders bunched tight beneath the pale skin.

"Don't be ridiculous. Those raiders would have cut us both to ribbons if you hadn't been here." Talia laid one slim brown hand between Rhin's shoulder blades, doing her best to exude calm. "And you can stop it with the 'Mersa' nonsense. We're not at the keep now."

"It isn't proper," Rhin protested. Talia stifled a laugh.

"It's a little late for us to worry about proper, love. Now hold still."

Rhin obeyed, but made a pained sound in her throat as Talia peeled off her leggings. A gash ran down the back of one powerful thigh, shallow but awkwardly-placed. She'd need stitches later. For now, Talia cleaned the wound as best she could and tore a strip of fabric from her skirts to wrap it.

"You're good at this," Rhin said, as she tied off the bandage. There was a touch of surprise in her voice.

Talia smiled. "And why shouldn't I be? I can take care of you too, you know."

A flush spread like a sunset down the back of Rhin's neck and across her shoulders. Talia trailed teasing fingertips up her side.

There was a moment when she thought Rhin would follow her lead, lean into the touch and let the morning's upset be banished. Then Rhin pulled away. "Raiders don't normally come this late."

Talia blinked at the non-sequitur. "What's your point?"

"The cold should have driven them off by now. This weather, it's…" Rhin gestured around—at the leaves still green upon the trees, the ground damp and giving beneath their feet, though it was certainly early enough in the day for frost. "Unnatural."

She had a point. Talia had worn her lightest cloak—the green-gold spring damask—and had stripped even that off as the morning wore on, sweaty from walking through the woods. "What do you suggest we do about it?" she asked.

"That's for your mother to decide." Rhin looked sideways at her. "But people are starting to talk. What if winter doesn't come this year? What if there's no ice blossom harvest?" She blinked rapidly. "What if the Cold God is angry with us?"

Talia squeezed her shoulder. "I don't think there's any point speculating about the gods. We deal with what we know. What we can see." She brought her free hand up to stroke Rhin's cheek. "What's right in front of us."

Rhin held her gaze for a moment, then ducked her head and reached for her leggings. "We should get back. Warn your mother about the raiders."

She tugged on her clothes, turned, and began to limp back in the direction of the city. Talia sighed. Then she followed.

Everything had been quiet when they left, only the earliest of risers and the latest of drinkers shuffling along the cobblestones in the pre-dawn gloom. Now, an urgent buzz of voices rose from the streets.

Rhin drew herself up, right hand going to her sword-belt. Her gait steadied, her limp banished, though holding it at bay had to be a painful effort. "Is something happening in the square today? I wasn't told."

Talia pursed her lips. "Nor I."

"We should take another route. Avoid the crowds. I may not be able to protect you right now."

"Who says there's anything to protect me from?" Talia kept her voice breezy, hoping she sounded more confident than she felt. "Let's investigate."

They wound through the streets, passing first stragglers, then knots of people, and finally throngs, singing and talking excitedly, all gravitating toward the same point. Not the keep, but the white stone temple of the Cold God in the main square.

Its pale columns reached straight and stark to its pointed roof. On the steps below, the High Priest stood with arms held aloft, head uncovered, draped in white furs. *Winter wears no crown,* proclaimed the archway above him, the first line of a popular invocation to the Cold God. Ice statues of former High Priests and Priestesses flanked the entrance on both sides, their eyes raised in prayer. Normally, their sharp-edged beauty showcased the artistry of the city's most talented sculptors. Today, they were already starting to melt, sweating away definition in the mild air.

"The Cold God has forsaken us." The priest's voice echoed around the square. "We must ask ourselves why. We must search our hearts, and the hearts of our neighbours…"

As Talia and Rhin threaded their way along the edges, glances followed them. Despite the morning sunshine, Talia drew the hood of her cloak up to shield her face and tucked her hands inside her sleeves to keep herself from fiddling nervously with her quartz pendant.

Rhin glanced toward the High Priest. "Do you want to hear what he has to say?"

She shook her head. "As you said, we should warn my mother about the raiders."

Though the streets around the keep were quieter, inside, they found the same anxious hum of activity. The same glances followed them—though here, eyes were politely averted as soon as they landed on Talia.

She collared a passing assistant. "My mother?"

His eyes flickered in the direction of the council chamber. "The Mers is with her advisors," he said. "If it can wait—"

"It can't." Talia swept toward the chamber. The heavy wooden doors were closed and guarded, but opened at her approach.

Talia's mother, robed in pale grey for the longed-for winter, sat on the far side of the room, a sheet of vellum on the table before her, Talia's stepfather at her right hand, and a knot of advisors clustered round them.

"There should be ice fields forming here by now," said one, finger stabbing at a point on the map. "And here. The harvest—"

The clack of Talia's boots on the stone floor made her mother look up. The advisor broke off, lips thinning.

Talia's mother gave her a sharp look. "Must you wear that colour at a time like this?" Pale green was a spring colour; an offence to the Cold God, according to some. It would discourage the snows and put off the winter harvest. Talia was never truly sure whether her mother put stock in such superstitions. She attended the temple and paid tribute to the Cold God, as every Mers did, but then, she needed the High Priest on side.

She huffed. "It's just a cloak, mother."

"It doesn't matter. People are nervous."

"I noticed." Talia planted her hands on her hips. "The streets around the temple were packed. The High Priest was out on the steps."

The advisor who'd spoken earlier frowned. "That's all we need. Spreading rumours, frightening people…"

Talia's mother threw her a warning look. "He's the voice of the Cold God, and has almost as much authority in this city as I do. We'll sow no discord." The woman fell silent, and the Mers turned to Talia. "Why are you here?"

"Raiders," she said, "in the woods to the south. We had an encounter."

"Are you hurt?"

"I'm fine." She inclined her head toward Rhin. "I had protection. Though Rhin will need someone to take a look at her leg."

Her mother's shoulders relaxed fractionally, and she gestured to the captain of the city guard. "Double patrols along the south-west wall, at least until the snows come." She turned back to Talia. "Go and change. And don't worry. Winter will be here soon."

She spoke with the finality of a door clanging shut, as she always did, suggesting she would brook no disobedience from the seasons or even from uncooperative gods. Only her eyes betrayed her unease.

Rhin woke in the night to the bright floral fragrance of Talia's bedsheets, scented each day with perfumed oils, and the embers of the wood fire dying in the grate. She stretched, lazily shedding sleep—and found the spot beside her cold.

Her hand flew to her waist, and then, once she'd remembered she was naked, to the side of the bed where she'd abandoned her sword last night. The movement pulled at her new stitches and she sucked in a sharp breath through her teeth.

"Over here, love." Talia's voice, weary.

Rhin made out her silhouette against the far window, almost swallowed by the dark. It was a clear night, the stars high and cold. Only their absence gave away her outline.

Ignoring the twinge in her thigh, Rhin climbed out of bed, pulling the heavy wool blanket over her shoulders. "Aren't you cold?" She padded across the room to wrap her arms around Talia from behind, enfolding them both in the blanket.

Talia hummed and leaned back into her embrace, but there was a tension in her narrow shoulders, fingers drumming the windowsill as she gazed out at the snowless landscape. "Not cold enough."

"I didn't expect you to be up worrying about it. You said there was no point."

She tried not to make it a reproach, but perhaps it was one, anyway. Talia turned in her arms, starlight catching the edges of her delicate profile. She looked, for a moment, as luminously distant as the ice statues that adorned the Cold God's temple.

"I said we should concern ourselves with what's in front of us." Talia flung one arm out, gesturing northward. "The gods stay locked in their mountain fastnesses, or they roam the skies, where we can't touch them. But their whims touch us. They *flatten* us. If the Cold God doesn't come, there'll be no harvest. Nothing to trade. Our people will starve. And there's nothing we can do, nothing *I* can do, except wear a stupid grey cloak and pretend he cares." She rubbed her temple. "That's why I can't stop thinking about it."

"I'm sorry," said Rhin.

A rueful smile. "Shouldn't you be lecturing me about how I need to have faith?"

Rhin held her tighter. "Somehow, I don't think it would help."

Talia allowed herself to be coaxed back to bed, and even slept, eventually, while Rhin lay awake.

Talia had grown up in the keep, where even in the dead of night there was noise somewhere. Rhin, raised in the deep quiet of her parents' northern stronghold, struggled with it even now.

At Godsfoot, the winter harvest came early—and life hung by the finest of threads. The presence of the gods breathed in the air. Nothing green grew up there; only the ice blossoms that made the Mersdom's fortune. Perfect and never-melting, they sold by the hundreds to southern nobles. Some said they sprang from the Cold God's footprints when he carried the source of his power, the Heart of Winter, through the land; others that they were a blessing he'd bestowed on the heroes of old, who'd made the pilgrimage to his icy fastness in the far north. Where Rhin came from, it was easy to believe it.

She'd felt the teeth of the north wind often enough to know their bite could only be divine wrath. She'd watched fields of ice blossoms flower and known they were a blessing, a love colder and brighter and harder than human love—but love, nonetheless.

The ground should have been shining with them now, but her mother's last letter had spoken of a thin harvest even at Godsfoot. They'd have little to trade this winter—would have to survive the year on supplies put by in more prosperous times, salted and fermented things that tasted of meanness and tedium.

But at least they and their dependents would survive. Those who had no walls to protect them from the cold and no cellars to see them through would suffer. And when people suffered, it was only natural they'd look for someone to blame. The High Priest was canny, getting out ahead of it and removing himself from the firing-line, though the temple never turned down tribute.

Rhin glanced down at Talia, her perfect profile silhouetted against her white pillow, her lips soft and parted in sleep. If only she wouldn't insist on wearing green, on scorning the Cold God in public—but she was as sure of the gods' indifference as Rhin was of their scrutiny.

Talia stirred, turning onto her back. The moonlight caught the silver pendant she wore, a drop of clear quartz threaded through with silver, like the Heart of Winter in miniature.

And an idea offered itself, just as clear and just as bright.

The moment she'd thought it, Rhin tried to push it away. It was a blasphemy of the worst kind.

But the Cold God had already forsaken them. Soon, people would begin to look for a solution they could see, one they could reach. A human target for their anger and their fear.

For all her skill and training, Rhin was only one woman. She wouldn't be able to protect Talia from a city raised to boiling-point by the High Priest. But if the cold harvest came, he'd have no tinder to light.

She wavered almost until the night was done. But with grey fingers of dawn creeping past the horizon and the keep finally, mercifully silent, Rhin strapped on her sword-belt and slipped away.

The eight days' ride to Godsfoot passed in an aching blur, punctuated by the occasional pause to eat, to redress the wound on her thigh as best she could, and to stretch her protesting muscles. At the edge of her parents' lands, Rhin brought Fern, her stout black mare, to a halt. The ice fields, stretching out toward the dark, cragged shape of Godsfoot in the distance, shone as brightly as they ever had, but were almost empty. The ice lay all but uninterrupted for mile upon mile, a mirror for the distant stars.

The track she'd been following petered out here. She could go no further on horseback.

Carefully, she dismounted, shouldered her bag, and turned Fern's head toward Godsfoot. "Go on," she said briskly, and when that wasn't enough, administered a slap to the horse's flank.

Fern gave her an affronted look, but broke into a brisk trot in the direction of the stronghold. Her hoofbeats faded into silence. Rhin hugged herself, feeling that the cold had grown a little sharper.

But she'd come this far. She turned north.

She wouldn't be sure, later, when the cold in the air turned into something more than cold. She seemed to see it freeze, the air sparkling with crystals, and to feel its brightness on her skin, in her nostrils, clinging to her eyelashes. At some point, her scarf fell down from over her nose and mouth, and she didn't feel it. She breathed into her hands, ran her tongue over her lips and found them chapped and bleeding, but it was as if her face belonged to someone else.

Time stretched; became strange. She no longer knew how long she'd been walking. The sky darkened, lightened, and then seemed to turn black again before she'd fully noticed. At one point she realised she was sitting down, and her heart beat panic-fast as she forced herself to her feet, terrified by how close she'd come to freezing to death in the snow.

Who was she to think she could survive in the Cold God's land? A fool, that was who.

Her strength began to fail. She slipped and landed hard on one knee. Pain knifed through the joint, and she sucked in air through her teeth. The effort of standing seemed impossible.

Then she blinked her frozen lashes and saw Talia flash before her mind's eye, a dark and delicate figure wrapped in a cloak of gold and spring green. The murmurings of the advisors and the glares of the cityfolk followed her like a sentence.

Rhin levered herself to her feet and trudged ahead. When she could no longer trudge, she stumbled; and, at last, she fell forward.

She should've landed on her face in the snow. Instead, her palms hit a wall of something smooth and pale. She raised her head—and gasped.

This was it.

The place where mountains of ice rose from the ground. Deep inside them, the Cold God made his home.

The thought should have made her tremble. Perhaps it would have, if she'd been able to feel her fingers. But there was a thrill in it, too. There were the old stories about humans who had made pilgrimages to the far reaches of the world to meet the gods, but nobody Rhin knew of had done it. She'd be the first in generations.

She cut the thought off at the knees. That was hubris, and she was here for a purpose.

Rhin forced herself to move, feeling her way along the side of the mountain, testing the surface with frozen hands. She needed a way in.

Her fingertips caught on something, the barest of imperfections in the surface of the ice.

Some part of her had been expecting magic. An entrance that would slide away into nothingness at her touch, the mountain silently offering itself. Instead, she groped uselessly around the outline of the door while nothing happened.

This might be the land of the gods, but she was only human, and had only human means at her disposal. She put her shoulder to the mountainside and pushed.

Teeth gritted, muscles straining, Rhin felt sweat begin to bead on her forehead despite the cold. Her arms shook. She'd always been proud of her strength, of the ease with which she could swing a longsword; perhaps unseemly so. She'd been proud of the way it made Talia look at her. Here, it availed her nothing.

Perhaps this was the lesson of her journey. She'd sought to interfere in the affairs of the gods, and now she would meet her end battering herself against the mountain wall like an insect trapped in a lantern.

Still, she lifted her chin and shoved once more.

The door moved. Only an inch, but it moved.

Lungs screaming, Rhin squeezed her eyes shut and pushed harder.

Inside, she'd expected darkness, but the hollowed-out centre of the mountain shone with a whole cool rainbow of colours, lights flickering and dancing within the ice. The narrow corridor in which she found herself was bright as day, but quiet. Her exhausted breathing sounded louder than a winded horse's in the silence, and she felt sure some acolyte of the Cold God would emerge at any moment to drag her away.

Slowly, slowly, Rhin crept through the tunnels. The lights grew brighter as she made her way deeper into the mountain, and she chose to believe that meant she was on the right path.

As she walked and saw no sign of life, the thought of being caught melted away. A new fear, deep and formless, took its place.

The corridors became higher and wider, and at last one spat her out into a cavernous empty chamber whose size made her heart skip. It seemed she'd walked into the white vastness of a winter sky.

At one end sat a throne carved of ice; on a plinth beside it, shining so brightly she had to look at it through her fingers, something like a frozen star. The size of her fist and whiter than the moon. The Heart of Winter.

Rhin peered around cautiously, half-expecting icy legions to materialise from nowhere, but she was alone.

Perhaps Talia had been right after all. The Cold God had abandoned them, not out of affront at any human slight, but for obscure reasons of his own.

Heart sinking, she trudged toward the throne. At least the Heart of Winter was still here. She might yet do some good.

She ascended the dais and reached for the Heart with trembling fingers. What would it feel like to touch it? Would it burn even through her gloves, or be like smooth, cool quartz?

For the space of a heartbeat, she held it in her hand like an apple plucked from the bough. It felt scarcely possible that so bright and strange a thing could be in her possession, that her human hands could encompass all its power, but there it was.

All at once, it turned to water.

It ran in rivulets over the leather of her glove and trickled into her sleeve. Rhin's skin tingled where the water touched it, as if she'd grasped a nettle. Then the feeling was gone, and it seemed she'd never been holding anything at all.

She thought she might weep but no tears came, only a sucking emptiness in the cavity of her chest.

When Rhin found herself back in the snows of the far north, she couldn't tell how long she'd been away. The days had blurred into an undifferentiated mass. She knew only that the world felt… different. Sharper and more intense, the wind like needles, the fabric of her heavy clothing irritating her skin. As though a bandage had been ripped away, leaving her a raw wound.

The cut on her thigh, though, had stopped hurting.

As she trekked south, snow and ice gave way to greenery, bitter winds to unseasonal mildness. The warmth irritated as much as the cold had, clinging to her skin like a wet film she couldn't shake off. And beneath it all, always, the gnawing teeth of failure.

The gods alone knew how she was going to explain this to Talia.

She bit back a bitter laugh at the thought. The gods? Why would they care to know?

When she finally came home, she found the streets around the keep too quiet, the thud of her horse's hoofbeats in the silence setting her on edge.

In the distance, toward the city centre, the murmur of a crowd. As she drew closer it became a hum, a rising tide. Rhin rode toward it, realising as she wound her way through the streets its gravity was pulling her toward the Cold God's temple.

That could mean nothing good.

Last time she'd watched the High Priest address the crowd outside the temple, his words had carried the gravity of absolute truth. They'd struck fear into her heart, for Talia and for the city. Now, his voice echoed through the streets but rang hollow. She rounded the corner into the square with a sneer.

The high priest stood atop the temple steps, hands gesturing, mouth open in oratory. Beside him was Talia, her wrists bound behind her, the dark shining ringlets of her hair dishevelled, her spring-green cloak falling off one shoulder.

She stood straight, chin up, face set in defiance. Nobody would see fear in the glitter of her eyes and the downturn of her mouth. Nobody but Rhin.

"The Cold God is angry," said the priest. "He withholds his presence from us. His cold harvest. And why is he angry, hm? We have our answer. Look at the contempt of those we allow to lead us! No wonder the God has forsaken us! We must offer a sacrifice."

At this, Talia stiffened. As good as a flinch, to Rhin's eyes.

"No!" It broke out of her involuntarily, startling her. She hadn't known her voice could be so loud, like the roar of the north wind.

All across the square, eyes turned in her direction. Her hand went to the hilt of her sword, a reflexive gesture. At the same time, she saw Talia's eyes go huge with shock, her pretence of calm momentarily abandoned.

Movement all around the square. Armed men and women—the Mers's guard—moved into fighting stances. Where were Talia's parents?

Had the balance of power shifted while Rhin had been gone? Had Talia's mother been ousted, imprisoned?

Or, worse, had she allowed this?

Rhin squashed the thoughts down. She was outnumbered. Even she couldn't fight her way past all those armed guards—and with the square packed with civilians, it would be dangerous even to try.

The calculation was simple enough. There was one way to save Talia. One way she could do something for them all, after the distraction of her foolish quest. "Take me as a sacrifice. I volunteer."

If Talia said anything, Rhin didn't hear it. The noise of the crowd had become a tidal wave. Then the guards were on her, and the ringing in her ears drowned it out.

They tied her to a tree on the north side of town. The High Priest lit a fire and ritually doused it; spoke an incantation to the Cold God.

*Winter wears no crown. Winter holds no lands.*

*Winter cares not for beauty; it asks no hand.*

*Winter drinks no wine. Winter eats no meat.*

*But winter has an appetite, and it has teeth.*

Once, Rhin had thought it a caution against presuming to understand the Cold God, or to persuade him with prayer. He was not human, and could not be swayed by the things of the mortal world.

How foolish she'd been. How much truer it was than she'd known.

But, as smoke rose from the embers, she felt a prickle of brightness on her skin, that same beyond-cold feeling that had gripped her as she approached the mountain.

Had she been wrong? Was the presence of the gods still here, in some small way? Would the Cold God come for his sacrifice after all? A tight knot of fear began to form in her gut.

At last the High Priest and his acolytes trooped away, the crowd drifting after them in twos and threes. Dusk came. And then a rustle among the trees. Soft footsteps.

Rhin squinted in the dark, not daring to hope. "Talia?"

A shape moved slowly into view, then rushed to her side. Talia rose onto her toes, pressing their foreheads together.

"Where have you been?" Talia breathed. "What happened?" She cut herself off. "Never mind that. I need to get you out of here." She took a step back, moving behind Rhin, fumbling with the bindings that dug into her wrists.

"Talia," Rhin said. "Stop."

Talia let go, went very still. "What?"

Rhin had never spoken to her like this before. "What will happen if the High Priest comes back in the morning and I'm gone?"

"It won't matter. We'll be far away from here by then."

"And he'll come after us. After you. He already held a grudge. This will make it worse."

"So I'm to let you risk your life instead?"

Rhin gave her a curious look. "You think it's a risk? Before I left, you were sure the gods cared nothing for what we did."

Talia huffed. "I'm not saying they care. I just don't think we can assume they'll refuse an offering. Winter has an appetite, remember?" She paused. "Anyway, last time we spoke, you were convinced they were listening to everything we did. What changed, Rhin?"

Rhin hung her head. "It's a long story."

"Well, we don't have long. So tell me fast."

Rhin bit her lip. "I—I went north. The day after we walked in on your mother with her advisors. I was afraid you'd talk me out of it, or just order me not to go."

A pained smile. "I would certainly have tried. But I wouldn't have forced you. You don't belong to me, love."

Rhin's chest hurt. "I wouldn't mind that, you know."

"I know," Talia sighed, her fingers curling in Rhin's yellow hair. "Where did you go?"

"As far north as I could."

"Home?"

"Past that. I found—Mersa, I found the Cold God's stronghold." Rhin fought back the urge to weep again. "He wasn't there. And I found the Heart, and— Now it's not there, either."

Talia stared. "What do you mean?"

"It melted in my hands, like snow." Rhin wished her hands were free so she could rub at her aching temples. "If anyone has wronged the Cold God, it's me, not you. That's why you have to leave me."

"I won't. The High Priest can rot."

She made her voice as gentle as she could. "But he won't. He has followers, armed guards. There's no use you sacrificing yourself as well."

"I have no intention of dying." Talia squared her shoulders. "There are still people loyal to my mother. They got us out of the city when the High Priest's acolytes came for me and took her south. There are places to hide there. They only found me because I came back to—" She cut herself off.

Rhin wished she could take Talia's hands in her own. "To look for me."

Talia gave a brisk little shake of her head. "Anyway, my mother thinks I'm still searching, and she won't leave without me. I'll go to her, get help." She lifted her chin. "Then I'll come back for you."

"There isn't time for that, Mersa," Rhin told her, softly.

Talia's eyes blazed. "I'll make time."

Rhin almost believed she could.

She pressed a final kiss to Rhin's lips and slipped back into the trees, and then Rhin was alone with the night. She watched the clear sky, an ocean of stars that seemed it would never end. But end it did, with the greying light of dawn, and the Cold God had not come.

The weak sun crept above the horizon and Rhin sagged in her bonds. If her transgression had been the thing that caught the Cold God's attention, bringing him back to them, it would have been worth dying.

But this? She wasn't even sure what they'd do to her now. Hang her, probably.

There was a crack like somebody stepping on a branch in the woods behind her. Not Talia and her reinforcements. They'd have made their presence known, instead of sneaking up. Rhin held her breath, ears straining. The High Priest, here to finish her off before the cityfolk arrived so he could claim his sacrifice had been accepted? Or even the Cold God in mortal guise, come to claim her at last?

She caught movement from the corner of her eye. Shapes detached themselves from the dark of the woods and took form in the murky dawn.

Then came the softly metallic sound of a blade being drawn, and its tip pressed against Rhin's throat. Her pulse rabbited beneath the sharp point, a smaller, far more familiar fear flooding through her.

"What have we here?" said a voice. "The Mersa's pet, trussed up all pretty for us?"

A leering figure moved into her field of vision. Its clothes told her the person was from the larger kingdom to the west—the one from which raiders came. Rhin's ears told her perhaps a dozen others surrounded her.

She'd maimed three of their number the morning she and Talia were attacked. At least one of those couldn't have survived his wounds. And raiders were nothing if not vengeful. The cold steel at her throat promised a wretched, helpless little end. One that would mend nothing, mean nothing.

Her last shard of hope snapped like an icicle crushed underfoot, and the fear was gone with it.

Something flooded out from the core of her. Cold; cold deeper than a winter's night. It reached down to her fingertips, an ache like starlight, and blazed behind her eyes. It was in every part of her, it *was* her, and she felt that she would burst with it, a supernova of ice exploding across the dawn sky.

The bonds that held her snapped as easily as a frozen cobweb.

The raider's eyes went wide, and the point of his sword broke the skin at her throat.

It didn't hurt, exactly. She was just aware of it, distantly, as if she'd grown some new protective layer.

Seemingly of its own accord, her hand gripped the blade. The raider took good care of his weapon, and its edges were sharp—but the cold was sharper, and the blade shattered like spun glass. The raider opened his mouth to shout a warning that never came out. A heartbeat later he'd gone still, his skin taking on a wintry grey tinge beneath Rhin's fingertips. He toppled to the ground, limbs rigid, quite dead.

His companions didn't wait for an encore. They scattered into the trees.

Rhin breathed out heavily, the strength leaving her, and leaned back against the broad trunk of a tree at the forest's edge. Vaguely, she was aware of the rough bark, of the sun rising before her and the wind stirring in the forest canopy. For a long time, that and the emptiness inside her were all there was.

After a time, she heard new footsteps among the trees and tensed, turning to face them. Perhaps the raiders had returned with reinforcements.

Talia stood before her, breathing hard. "You're safe," she gasped, and then a frown drew her brows together. "No, you're hurt." She reached for Rhin's throat, for the place where the raider's sword had broken the skin.

"I'm fine." Rhin shied back. "Don't touch me." Hurt clouded Talia's face, and Rhin had to fight the urge to take her hand. "I don't want to hurt you."

"What do you mean?" Talia frowned. "You look... different."

"I feel different." She drew a breath; took in the wondering, wide-eyed way Talia was looking at her.

Sudden, inexplicable hope flickered to life inside her, a cold flame.

"Stand back." Rhin stepped away from the treeline, toward the expanse of damp grass that should have been blooming with ice blossoms by now. She crouched and pressed the fingers of her right hand into the ground.

Cold bloomed from her touch like a ripple on the surface of a lake. The ground froze with it, clear as glass and gleaming in the morning sun.

Something pushed its way out of the ice—a tiny fractal of white, like a furled rose.

The first ice blossom of the winter.

Rhin leaned forward to pluck it, cradling it carefully in her palm. She took a moment to marvel at the delicate edges of its petals, its perfect symmetry. Then she rose to her feet and turned back, holding it out.

Wordlessly, Talia took the ice blossom. Her eyes were wet with tears.

"They're afraid of me." Rhin had noticed it as soon as they made their return to the city. People looked at her differently now, and not just those who'd followed the High Priest. He was in a cell, and most of his followers had drifted away, though the faithful still clustered around the temple steps.

Occasionally, someone would pluck up enough courage to ask Rhin to bless them, and that was worse. She missed the days when the only power she wielded was in her muscles and her sword.

Talia—wearing sturdy leather gloves—laced their fingers more tightly together. "They don't know you, that's all."

"I'm not sure I know myself anymore." Rhin had begun dreaming of places she'd never been. Icy wastes beyond even the frozen mountain, winds howling between the stars. Inhuman places where no-one could follow her.

Talia stopped; pulled Rhin to her in the crowded square, careless of who was watching. "I know you. And I know the Cold Goddess will be far kinder than the Cold God."

Rhin winced. "Don't call me that, Mersa. Please."

"Don't call me *that* and we have a deal."

That pulled a small smile from Rhin, despite herself. "I think I can manage that."

"Good." Talia slid her hand from Rhin's grasp and pulled off her leather glove.

"Mer— My love?"

"If you want this to work, you're going to have to trust me." Talia regarded her sternly. "And yourself."

Rhin hesitated, fingers trembling. It took her a moment to steady herself, but she reached out. Talia took her hand.

There was a brief flash of cold, like scooping up a handful of snow, and then it was gone. Talia's pulse beat strong and steady beneath the skin, and her touch was warm as spring.

*JL George lives in Cardiff and writes weird and speculative fiction. Her work has appeared in Fireside, Cossmass Infinities, Curiosities, and various other magazines and anthologies, and her first novel The Word is out now. In her other lives, she's a library-monkey and an academic interested in literature and science and the Gothic.*

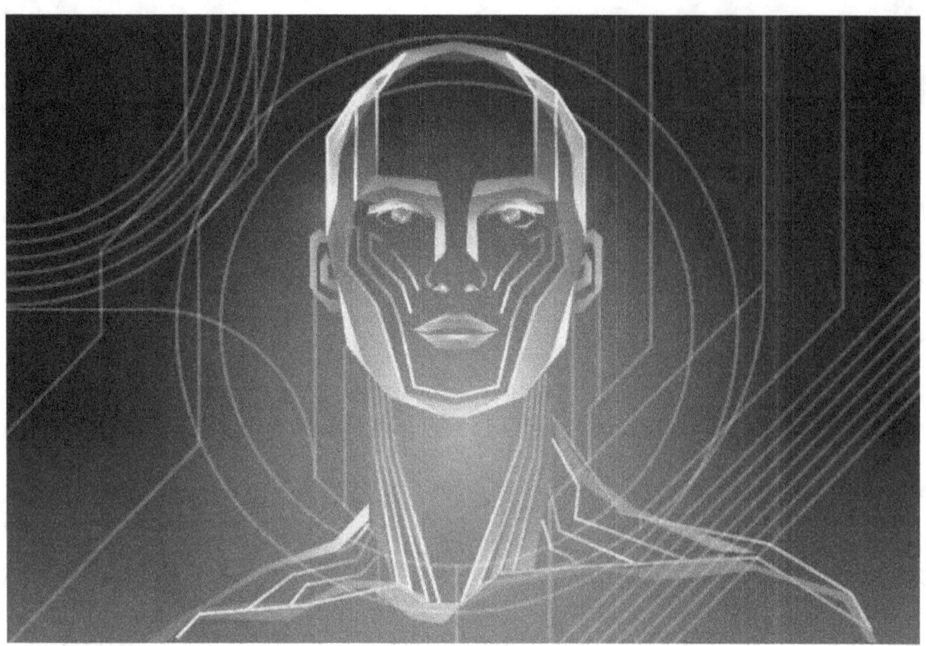

# The Secret
## *Michael Teasdale*

Tilda peered down through the sun-tinted windows of the limousine as it sliced through the heat haze of the azure sky. Despite the celebrity of her fellow passenger, she remained largely detached from his presence, marvelling at the intersecting shards of steel and glass that rose from the acrid sand like the grasping tentacles of a great crystalline leviathan. She felt the ascent in her belly, restraining her giddiness as the limo climbed, quickening, to its destination, weaving past the towering hologram of Sheik Zayed that stood, translucent and benign, smiling down over the tracks of the hyperloop. Far below, Tilda could make out the gleaming metallic pods that arced across the desert, shuttling lesser mortals along their daily commute. On any other Friday, she would have been down among them, hot and tired instead of enjoying the paradise of the tiny silver bullet that now carried her into a different stratosphere of wealth and privilege.

As if to rouse her from her distraction, the limo banked to the left and began its descent. Great bursts of concentrated steam announcing its arrival as the craft came to rest on the rooftop of the Burj Al Arab.

The door popped opened, sliding up into the interior of the craft and Tilda watched as her companion, a dapper gentleman in an expensive ice-cream coloured suit, oddly punctuated by a crude enamel pin-badge, stepped out and waited patiently for the blank faced robot to trundle across the rooftop and bid him a good day.

"As-salamu alaykum, Mr. Nemeth." said the robot in a metallic tone that, nevertheless, carried impeccable pronunciation.

The well-dressed man smiled, although his eyes remained hidden behind the dark lenses of his sunglasses. "Wa alaykumu as-salam." he replied, with somewhat less convincing authenticity. He reached over to the door, offering his hand to Tilda. "Miss Lillvik, welcome to my world."

Tilda took Nemeth's hand, clutching her All-Purpose-Device with the other and planting one foot on the rooftop, as he helped her out of the craft. His grip felt clammy and loose and she noted the small beads of sweat which had already begun to form on his brow. Her heels had barely settled in the scattered dust of the landing pad, before the mid-day heatwave hit her and almost sent her reeling back into the cool oasis of the limo.

*"Jävla fan!"* she cursed in her native tongue then readjusted. "Wow…it's…a little warm."

Her gaze flicked to the porcelain white shell that masked the robot's face and she shuddered despite the heat. *These ghoulish things again*, she thought. *That horrible lack of detail.*

The hollow black eyes stared back at her as the robot addressed her directly. "As-salamu alaykum, Miss Lillvik. It is 52.1º Celsius today." It turned to her companion "that's 125.78º Fahrenheit to you, Mr. Nemeth. May I please lead you to the elevator, in order to avoid any further discomfort?"

Nemeth grinned, flashing the pearly whites that Tilda knew to be both absurdly expensive and entirely artificial, and tugged at the lapels of his jacket. "Lead away." he beamed, gesturing to Tilda. "After you, *min kära*." he smiled.

His Swedish was no more convincing than his Arabic but she forced herself to return the gesture.

*He's something of an ass,* she thought, *but I guess humility doesn't make anyone a billionaire.*

Stepping into the elevator she waited, breathing a quiet sigh of relief as Nemeth dismissed the robot, which wheeled away into a shaded part of the rooftop. As the doors hissed close, Nemeth removed his sunglasses and wiped the sweat from the bridge of his nose, letting his famously enigmatic gaze fall directly on her for the first time that day.

"Floor 27 please." he said, addressing the elevator. Then he smiled at her. "Not a fan of them, are you?" he asked and then, as if suddenly remembering something more important, immediately changed the subject "Did you know they have a solid gold bar here?"

Tilda dismissed the second question, more interested in the accusatory nature of the first. "A fan of who?" she asked.

The elevator hummed and began its whisper-quiet descent.

"Not a gold bar like the type you get in pirate stories," said Nemeth, lost in his own train of thought, "a drinks bar…made almost entirely of gold. Ludicrously ostentatious of course but then we are in …sorry, what?"

"I'm not a fan of who?" Tilda clarified.

"Oh," Nemeth smiled and he pointed upwards. "The robots. My wonderful automatons." He smiled, fidgeting with pin badge on his lapel. "I'm afraid you'll have to get used to them here. The Crown Prince is a big fan, you know!"

Tilda frowned. "It's just…why do they look so…unfinished? That blank face? It's like something out of an old sci-fi movie. I guess I don't understand why you choose to make them that way when your tech is capable of…I mean…I've seen the working prototypes. We covered them extensively in NemCorp's early days. They looked…well…"

"Human?" offered Nemeth.

The elevator pinged and a crystal-clear speaker hummed into life. "We have arrived at Floor 27. Home of the *Gold on 27*. Have a pleasant stay Mr. Nemeth. Jag önskar er en trevlig vistelse, Miss Lillvik."

Nemeth grimaced and pointed up at the speaker. "Now that's what gives *me* the creeps." He cringed. "The robots? Not really. There's a good reason for their design. Let's freshen up with a drink and I'll explain. Did I mention they have a solid gold bar here?"

Tilda knew all about the bar. She knew everything about Nemeth; his haunts and his history. From his impoverished upbringing in England following the death of his father, to the way he would find solace in code. She knew about his troubled school days, his years in community college. She had personally spoken to embittered former colleagues who had flipped burgers with him during his time as a college drop-out and had remained flipping burgers long after his own personal star had soared, propelling him first to the tech havens of California and to his ultimate residency here in to the tax haven of Dubai. His litany of past relationships, mostly short and complicated, were widely documented as were his battles with substance abuse and infidelity. Yet none of these outliers ever seemed to derail the perfect algorithm that had been his phenomenal rise to success. A darling of the industry, his company, NemCorp, had, in little more than a decade, become the undisputed giant of artificial intelligence, funded heavily, it

was rumoured, by the Crown Prince himself.

All of this, Tilda knew. As a journalist it was her job to know. But this particular assignment went beyond the simple magazine profiles she had written in the past. Nemeth wasn't just another billionaire. Increasingly, he was seen as hope for what a billionaire *could* be. Despite the huge debate over the regimes that he lived and worked among he was nevertheless viewed as somewhat of an ethical magnate. A man of pointed ideals with an altruistic mission for humanity that extended beyond the usual self-centred egotism.

It was a shame, thought Tilda, that, so far, she wasn't seeing any of this. Instead, it was all as depressingly familiar as the other tycoons she had developed a reputation for profiling. There was a narcissism that bled through the chain-link armour of his quiet humble-bragging. A desperate need for validation, common among his kind, lay buried in his roots. The only real challenge was finding the right tool for the excavation. In Nemeth's case, it evidently came in the form of a frosted glass. He was three Bombay Sapphires into 'freshening up', jacket off, sleeves rolled up over his hairy forearms, when Tilda finally circled him back around to the topic raised in the elevator.

Nemeth sipped his drink. "People." he began "We are afraid. Afraid of things that look like us but…aren't. You've heard of 'uncanny valley', I'm sure? Nothing to do with Silicon Valley…although…I guess it kind of is, given who we're talking about."

She knew exactly what he was talking about but shook her head, playing dumb for him anyway. Explaining well-known phenomena to female journalists was another thing that billionaires seemingly enjoyed.

"There's something primordial. An evolutionary response. Like how we'll still flinch from a common spider long after we know they aren't a threat. Some part of us…it remembers. Some primal memory takes us back to a time when those spiders were a big deal. It's the same deal with the robots. We created them. They're perfectly safe. We know this because we coded them, after all. But something drives us to fear close replicas of ourselves. Probably it's a survival instinct, meant to stop cavemen mating with their cousins…" he winced at the analogy "I'm sorry," he said, looking down at the glass of crystal-blue gin as if it were somehow responsible.

Tilda, broke the tension with a little laugh. "Well, no chance of anyone wanting to mate with one of those." she smiled, pointing out the robot stationed by the door.

Nemeth stopped examining his glass and his smile faded. "That's not the only fear. There's something else, isn't there? A deeper concern." his eyes drifted into the middle-distance. "We're frightened that eventually, they'll replace us."

It made sense. Ever since the dawn of the industrial revolution, humans had been gripped by a vague paranoia over new technology. Factory workers had frowned at the introduction of conveyor belts and autonomous machinery and their concerns had ultimately been validated. Computers that could perform, in mere nano-seconds, complex calculations that had once taken talented people days to crack, had added to mankind's collective anxiety. The response had been to challenge them in increasingly ludicrous displays. A human chess champion defeating a computer was greeted with all the zealous tubthumping of an overbearing father besting his infant son at tennis. It was preposterous, yet somehow justified. Tilda thought of the limo they had taken to the roof of the Burj Al Arab. Only a few decades ago it would have needed a driver and certainly wouldn't have been capable of whisking them to a rooftop destination one thousand feet from the desert floor. Fifty years ago, the very concept would have been the stuff of sci-fi, mocked as unrealistic even as a half-baked fantasy of the future. Now, here it was, existing as an ordinary part of life for Dubai's super rich.

"So, what you're saying is that you keep the design basic to make them more acceptable to the public? *Less* scary?" she asked. She glanced again at the smooth blank face of the greeter and shuddered. "It's not working for me." she laughed.

Nemeth shrugged. "It's not my call, obviously. I didn't choose the final design. The wheels are also not my preference when we have the tech to give them perfectly functioning legs. Even acknowledging why it's done; I think we could spare a little more detail on the face but…it is what it is. It's fitting in a way, because that's what that face is: a shell. A protective cover to make people feel safe about what might be going on inside."

Tilda leaned in. She could smell the gin on Nemeth's breath and his eyes seemed to be considering something deeply. "And what *is* going on inside?" she said in a low conspiratorial tone. "Consciousness?"

Almost as soon as the word left her lips, she recognised her mistake.

Nemeth lowered his gaze to the All-Purpose-Device by her side, its LED blinking green. "Is your APD still connected?"

She nodded and picked it up. "It is," but I can turn it off if it would make you feel more comfortable."

**Nemeth drained his drink, waved a finger at the bartender, and nodded.**

Tilda deactivated the APD and felt the slight twinge in her temple. It was a new device running the latest firmware and still causing a little discomfort with her implant. If Nemeth noticed, then he didn't remark upon it and seemed to take her on trust. After all, she'd been shadowing him all morning and the arrangement had been worked out over several months, where both she and her commissioning editor had been meticulously scrutinized in advance. Given her reputation for positively reporting on the motivations of other billionaires in the past, the vetting process had, this time, been unusually thorough. Nemeth, so it seemed, was a more suspicious type than most.

The prospective arrival of a fresh drink seemed to swing him back to a more positive mood while Tilda continued to cradle the sole blueberry and ginger sour she had first ordered half an hour ago.

"Now, you see," said Nemeth, smiling at the altogether more human bartender who stood shaking up a margarita a foot away from them. "This is a profession that doesn't have to worry." He winked back at her. "Nobody would trust a robot to mix a cocktail as good as these."

She took a reluctant sip of her own drink, letting the sugar around the rim crackle on her teeth as she glanced around the bar and its absurd golden furnishings. It was time to steer the conversation in a different direction.

"You mentioned the elevator making you shiver. Why was that? Because of how it identified us?"

Nemeth nodded. "It's simple slight-of-hand stuff really. Old-fashioned facial recognition tech tied to our bookings and a multi-lingual greeting algorithm. But it's a reminder, all the same."

"Of what, exactly?"

Nemeth's eyes shifted around the room, then back down to the All-Purpose-Device.

"Of *those* things." He muttered and knocked back the last of his gin. "Of how much of our data we've surrendered freely to the cloud. The tracking, the…" he seemed hesitant to use the word, "the profiling. All of our habits and interests. Our voices, their tics and mannerisms. The stories we tell one another." A grave expression fell over his face. "This is what we should be afraid of, not the outward appearance of an automaton, but what can be cloned behind that face. It's the combination of the two that should trouble us, because at what point will we struggle to separate the real from the artificial?" He rubbed the bridge of his nose again as if waking from a dream. "It doesn't put you ill at ease?" he asked. "As someone who makes their living reporting on people like me?"

Tilda frowned. It wasn't an avenue she had ever considered and the realisation stung a little. Most of the advancements in cloud-tech and cerebral implants had come long before she was born. The decision to have her linked was made at birth, as it was for most children, by her parents. She had yet been given cause to regret it, or even consider the possible negative ramifications of their choice. She certainly hadn't expected to be challenged on it for the first time by a billionaire tech boss. Being cloud-linked had given her access to a world of information from childhood. She couldn't imagine what it must be like for the 10% of the population who still refused the implant, opting to live in a disconnected stone-age of laborious manual research and old-fashioned education. She had always regarded the luddites as little more than deranged conspiracy theorists. After all, how could denying children freedom of access to information over some vague paranoia do anything but stunt their educational growth during the crucial formative years. Yet now, locked in the gaze of an eccentric billionaire, she had…what exactly? Doubts?

Nemeth smiled.

"I can see we disagree. Maybe you're surprised to find that someone who made his money through tech could hold sympathy with the luddites, but I don't like the power it affords to those who control the cloud. The degree to which they can use it to shape our lives…to socially engineer us and…that thing is definitely turned off, right?" he added, looking down at the APD with concern.

Tilda smiled back at him. She hadn't been expecting such vulnerability. This was good, it was an angle. The first lines of the article were beginning to write themselves.

"Can I tell you, now that we're speaking off the record, what my greatest pleasure in life is?" Nemeth grinned.

Tilda raised an eyebrow. Her research had already given her some ideas.

Nemeth waved away her thought with a stroke of his hand and thanked the waiter as he delivered a fresh drink. "Not that," he said "it's something much more…primal."

"I'm still not sure I need to hear this." Tilda giggled. A calculated response. This was exactly what she wanted to hear.

"Secrets." said Nemeth "I enjoy our capacity to keep them" he waved a hand at the sleeping device "despite those things." His eyes sparkled as if he were fondly recalling the sweet hiraeth of a place he could never return to. "We have so few secrets anymore. Almost everything we do is tracked and uploaded to the cloud; the rest can be easily extrapolated. So, I hold on to that earlier time. Those memories from before…before the decision was taken for me. The bits only I know…and sometimes…sometimes I like to share them…for fun."

The realisation hit Tilda like a wave. *Of course,* she thought *that's why he has this paranoia, he grew up without the implant. His parents must have been luddites; anti-cloud. That's why his father coded on those beat-up old machines. The same machines that were passed on to his son. That's why he holds the robots back. Keeps them basic: easily identifiable. He's afraid. He's deathly afraid of what they could become.*

Nemeth drained the drink then smiled at her.

"I'm famished." he announced. "Let's eat."

They didn't speak again for close to a decade after that drunken meal. Long after the dust had settled on what turned out to be a more controversial article than either of them had been expecting.

The call came in the early hours of the morning; Cross-continental, waking Tilda from a sleep that a daughter who hadn't existed during their last meeting, rarely let her enjoy uninterrupted.

The smart home AI jolted her awake, announcing the call in its cold feminine voice.

"Tilda, du har et inkommande samtal från …"

There was a change in tone and a gruff male voice slurred a familiar name.

Tilda sat up in bed, yawning and rubbing her bleary eyes as her mind danced back to the last time that she'd heard the voice. The memory of Nemeth's sparkling blue eyes briefly lit up the darkness.

"Vill du svara, Tilda?" asked the AI.

"Ja..." she said, then mentally switched to English. "Yes, but Screen off!" she added.

A lime green holo-projection shimmied into focus giving vague illumination to the room. The nodes danced as his voice rolled through.

"Miss Lillvik, I hope it's not too early. This is Roger...Roger Nemeth. Your number was...difficult to find. Congratulations on that."

More apologies followed while she rubbed her bleary eyes and turned on the nightlight. The sun that Swedes had once longed for during cold winters had now become an unwelcome harbinger that, at this hour, remained mercifully asleep, along with the rest of the sensible folk of Stockholm.

"It occurred to me, this morning, that it's been almost a decade and I wanted...I wanted to clear the air...to see if we could...maybe meet, for a fresh interview." He was slurring...drunk or suffering the effects of something else.

Tilda, smoothed back her greying hair, visibly adjusting to the disembodied voice as if Nemeth had stepped suddenly out from her wardrobe, still wearing the freshly laundered ice-cream-suit that would have been hopelessly impractical today.

"Mr. Nemeth. I'm surprised." She said, bluntly. "Your representatives didn't seem too happy with the direction that our last interview took."

From across the line, she heard a sigh and the nodes of the projection trembled.

"That...that wasn't your fault. You did your job. It was on me to keep my...concerns to myself. In a way, I'm glad you talked about them and... it's not like you ever betrayed the secret I told you. I appreciate that, in any case."

She had known, even as she'd typed it, that the article, framed around Nemeth's speculation on AI and his anxieties over the cloud and personal privacy, would light a fire under the tech-world. Already perceived as a different breed of billionaire it made him something of an unwilling spokesman to the sceptics and fuelled intense debate over the future of robotics and the ethics of cloud connection. His reputation as the anti-hero fighting from within the 1% had only been bolstered, but to his backers this mattered little, instead making him formidable enemies among the power circles he walked among. The Crown Prince, in particular, was rumoured to have been furious, believing that the article should have focussed on NemCorp's presence in the UAE, rather than exposing its founder's personal paranoia over the dangers of the tech that his own company manufactured. In the years that followed, Nemeth had drifted out of favour in the Arab world, taking up residence once again in California, where the outdoor temperature was slightly more bearable...although, these days, not by much.

"Listen, I want you to meet me. I'll be in Chicago next week for the migration summit. I figured you'd be there in any case. I have a room at The Drake. There's something I need to talk to you about in person...because I know...I know now that you can keep a secret."

He sounded scared.

Tilda straightened as her mind cast back to that dinner almost a decade ago and the bizarre secret that he had shared with her, she heard the words leaving her lips. She saw the entry flash into her calendar on the holo-projector. She spent the rest of the day in a whirl, arranging childcare, explaining to her staff at *Aftonbladet* why she would be taking an unexpected leave of absence. Finally, all loose ends accounted for, she boarded the jet that Nemeth had paid for to whisk her away to Chicago, where, in a matter of days, the US summit on what was being deemed the 'Great Migration' was due to take place.

Tilda arrived to find the protests at their peak and a city figuratively, if not yet literally, on fire.

Every country had its own take on the proposed interplanetary migration plan. While regressive insular republics like England and North Korea made plans to remain and deal with the consequences of the climate emergency, the majority of the world was already making plans for departure.

Her own home country of Sweden was part of a rapidly expanding socialist alliance encompassing their Scandinavian neighbours along with much of Eastern Europe. While the logistics were still being fine-tuned, there was no talk of leaving anyone behind against their will to suffer the grim fate that now seemed inevitable.

She thought back to the heatwave that had hit her that day in Dubai, when she had first stepped out of the limo and onto the roof of the Burj Al Arab, and how, a decade later, simply standing in that same spot would have been almost impossible without portable shielding. Even here, in Chicago, the temperature wasn't much less tolerable than it had been on that day ten years ago. The wildfires were burning across the west coast and it wouldn't be long before the streets were aflame, not yet from the man-made apocalypse, but from public outrage over America's all too predictable response to it.

"Peak Capitalism!" a visibly aged Nemeth groaned as they sat in the hotel room. "The future of humanity, surrendered into the hands of private enterprise. The elevation of the privileged few over the needs of the many. This is what it all boils down to, Miss Lillvik. Quite literally. This is the end game of everything they've been working towards."

It was a curious monologue delivered by an improbable player and Tilda felt almost duty bound to interject.

"You don't feel responsible?"

Nemeth smiled and nodded.

"More than you can imagine, *min kära*, and this is why I find myself here today, an honoured guest as the rest of my kind gather to discuss how best to monopolise the future of our species on an interstellar level. But let's get real for a moment; I know what I am to them. What I've always been to them…" he trailed off.

"And what exactly is that?" probed Tilda.

Nemeth bristled. "An outsider. Someone who stumbled into their little club one day and made himself useful, but was never really born to be among them. I'm fine with it. I accept absolutely what I am. My failures, my legacy. But I'm not as burned out and finished as they think." He thumped his fist into the palm of his hand. "You know, I'm often asked what the point of being a billionaire is and I've never really had an answer to it…but today, today I know. I've been keeping it secret. Just like the secret I shared with you all those years ago and now, because I know that I can trust you, because you never told anyone in close to a decade, I'm going to share with you my biggest secret. Don't worry, you won't have to hold onto it for long, because in twenty-four hours, those bastards are going to find out what happens when you let the wrong sort of person into the club!"

When the talking was over Tilda went back to her hotel room, powered on her virtual keypad and let her fingers dance in the air. She had less than twelve hours to deliver the scoop of her professional life before it became common knowledge and every news station on the planet was covering it.

Billionaires and private enterprise had been at the forefront of space travel for decades now. What most had assumed to be narcissistic self-indulgence had steadily emerged to be something far more sinister. The reality being proposed by the so called 'great migration' was exactly that, a lengthy mass-exodus of the Earth's populace to escape the irreversible decline of the one planet that had always been their home.

Terraforming, cyanobacteria, and a whole series of long-term proposals were already in play and the subject of intense international discussion; however these were long term solutions to the catastrophe of Earth's climate and, in the meantime, the most viable solution were the arks: Enormous, unprecedented spacecraft designed to support life for generations, while viable, liveable alternatives to Earth could be terraformed and colonised. Each country had a different approach with some banding together with close international allies, combining funding to form broad coalitions that could pool the cream of their science and tech industries into the project.

Others had rejected the idea completely, passing off the visible emergency that was the climate disaster as a piece of fiction and a work of fearmongering foreign powers looking for any excuse to colonise space in their own name.

The uniting problem for all countries was a simple one. There were just too many people to accommodate in the inaugural wave and so the decision needed to be taken; how would they prioritise?

The US had taken a predictable pattern in dealing with this, placing its own migration project into the hands of private enterprise. Corporations would fund and supply arks with the sole aim of selling placements to the rich. As for the poor and the middle class? *Well,* thought Tilda as she typed, *welcome to public healthcare: the sequel.*

*A decade ago,* wrote Tilda, *Nemeth dropped a virtual hand-grenade with incendiary comments that shook up the tech industry. His remarks caused millions to question, perhaps for the first time, our relationship with AI. His latest plan may just as well equate to an atom bomb being dropped on the carefully laid plans of private enterprise to monopolise an off-world future, accessible exclusively to the wealthiest citizens.*

Tilda's fingers hovered in the air, recalling Nemeth's words to her earlier that day. She envisaged him now, sitting in front of a room full of his fellow billionaires, dropping a second bombshell in the same rapid fire, excitable way he had revealed it to her.

"This is it." He had crowed "This is my purpose. This is the answer to the question of 'what do you need all that money for?' I'm going to use it to help people! I'm going to take all of NemCorp's assets and put it into public access arks. I'm going to give a free alternative to the poor and the needy. Give them the same chance to get off the planet as these cigar chomping sons of bitches! And the rich...they're going to come for me because of it. Maybe right away…I've an idea of how they'll do it…and that's why I'm telling you all of this Tilda, because if something happens…if something happens to me. You're the only one I can trust to get the truth out."

For a moment her fingers hovered over the keys, considering the words. Then they began to dance again and didn't stop until the article was complete.

When it was time for the press conference, Tilda switched off her APD and went dark. She wanted to absorb Nemeth's announcement here, from her hotel room, in real time, in the same authentic, unfiltered way that people, decades ago, would have witnessed the first Martian landings and other pivotal moments in humanity's history. Free of distraction, without the interruption of emoticon rainfall or rapid-fire feedback loops colouring her view. She didn't need to be there in person. Her exclusive was already wrapped, her questions answered directly by the man himself. It was ready to roll the second an official confirmation was made.

As a tribute to that first drunken bombshell ten years ago, she'd ordered a blueberry sour from room service and a service droid had brought it to her. A lot had changed in a decade. The people had begun to grow more and more accustomed to android tech. They were no longer the blank faced ghouls that had first spooked her at the Burj Al Arab. Now they looked visibly human, although NemCorp and its competitors kept a somewhat angular design to the faces, like a low-polygon render from an ancient videogame. People still wanted to tell the difference, after all. They still needed that same basic confirmation of droid inferiority. Nemeth had been wrong about one thing, thought Tilda, as she sipped from the glass and once more let the sugar crackle on her tongue; the robots could mix a great cocktail after all!

On the screen, an empty, miked up podium emblazoned with the logos of NemCorp and a dozen other multinational conglomerates stood waiting in an oak panelled room as the excited turmoil of the assembled reporters could be heard over the anchor's speculation.

And then, as the murmur rose to a crescendo, he arrived. Striding out onto the stage, flanked by a heavy-set security detail, flashing those hundred-thousand-dollar pearly whites as he strode up to the mic and began an announcement that would change everything.

"Hello ladies and gentlemen. My name is Roger Nemeth, founder and CEO of NemCorp…but then, you know that already."

Warm laughter rang out from the assembled press. Nemeth gave a wry smile.

"I stand before you today with an exciting offer to the American people. The history of this great nation is the history of a very special dream: that anyone, regardless of their background, creed or colour could come here and, with the right mindset and a little hard work, achieve all that they desired from life. The story of the United States of America is the story of immigrants, pioneers and most of all, it is the story of opportunity."

Tilda, glanced down at the deactivated APD then back at the screen.

"I myself came here as an immigrant to help found a company and build a dream. Now I want to extend an opportunity back to the American people. As our planet faces an unparalleled environmental crisis, our people once again ready themselves for a journey to a

New World. Yet, this time, it is the stars themselves that beckon us. I know that many of you face a perilous choice between the financial burden of joining the migration and concern over the sustainability of choosing to remain here, in the place that has always been our home."

Something was off. Tilda couldn't put her finger on it. There was Nemeth, the words all seemed to be heading in the right direction, but something about the tone, the cadence was wrong. The speech, of course, would have been written for him, yet somehow, even the opening joke rang hollow.

Her fingers stroked the deactivated APD. These days it was harder and harder to leave it off. Perhaps it was this anxiety making her paranoid. She downed the drink as Nemeth built to the climax of his speech.

"And so today, my friends, I want to extend an opportunity to you all. To give back hope to those who may feel that all hope is gone and that their chance has passed. It is my pleasure to introduce to you, what we at NemCorp are calling, the Lottery of the New Frontier."

Tilda's grip loosened and the empty glass tumbled to the ground, spilling half melted ice-cubes across the plush velvet carpet.

*What was this?*

She listened in a daze as Nemeth went on to explain himself. Rather than the grandiose plans to build fleets of public access arks he had outlined to her in the hotel room, Nemeth instead detailed a privately funded public lottery that would be held each week across the coming year. Every American citizen would be eligible to purchase a ticket and NemCorp would personally fund a placement for the lucky winners on one of the raft of private arks that were already being readied by its rival corporations.

Tilda understood. It was an opportunity that gave hope to every citizen but, in reality, its odds were no better than cleaning-up at the roulette table in Las Vegas. This was not the great hope of the poor and disenfranchised that he had extolled to her in the hotel room. It would provide safe passage to an insignificant number of people at best. Yet, she understood, that it was the hope that mattered. It was the hope that would quell the riots and give the people a distraction from reality…the reality that they were being abandoned, left behind to die in the figurative house fire that awaited all who remained.

It was a crock of shit.

A bill of goods.

Snake oil.

And Tilda hated him for it.

Grimacing she flicked on the APD and felt the pulse in her temple as the reactions began flooding her senses.

"What is this Tilda? We can't run this story now? Did he play you? Please call me as soon as you get this. I need to…"

She turned off the APD. The article…maybe even her reputation was ruined. Everything he'd told her. His plans to build enough arks to house the entire American underclass had been a lie. Instead, he was acting as a glib, talking head for a national pastime designed to do nothing but give false hope to millions, to keep them throwing money against the wall for the little time that remained before their paymasters could abort the planet and safely navigate their way clear of the pitchforks.

But why? Why even involve her in this? Was it really just a trivial bit of revenge for temporarily derailing his ride with the article she'd written almost a decade earlier? Was he so spiteful?

No. She couldn't countenance that she had misjudged him that badly. There had to be another explanation and yet, looking at the smiling, gesticulating man on the screen as he outlined the pantomime of his proposal, she felt nothing but blind fury towards him. She rose, ready to hurl her APD through the damned screen.

Then she froze.

The camera had pulled out and panned to the side a little, giving a full view of Nemeth as he stood at the podium. Her eyes lingered on the lapel of his jacket and her jaw fell open in horror as her mind flashed back to that drunken dinner ten years ago.

"There are two of them right now. The Crown Prince has one. He's already used it for several official engagements this year."

Tilda's jaw hung open then too. Not at the majesty of the Al Mahara restaurant and the floor to ceiling aquarium that offset their private table, but by the revelation Nemeth was openly dropping while a shoal of royal blue tangs darted by behind the plexiglass.

"Wait…in public?"

Nemeth smiled as he merrily cracked open the claw of a king lobster. "Not the first time, not the second or the third either. The Crown Prince is not one for trivial public appearances. It's less about security for him as it is the ability to escape tedious social engagements."

Tilda put down her fork. This was mindboggling beyond anything she had expected from Nemeth. It was also both frustratingly off the record and the kind of thing that, without evidence, would just as likely see her committed to an asylum as earn her a Pulitzer.

"Let me get this straight, you're telling me that the tech exists, right now, at NemCorp to produce an android that is virtually indistinguishable from its human counterpart?"

Nemeth popped a piece of lobster flesh into his mouth and chewed on it for a moment before replying.

"Not virtually indistinguishable." He said "Actually indistinguishable, as the Crown Prince's dinner guests would confirm, if only they knew."

"That's…" began Tilda, unsure how to finish.

"Terrifying." Agreed Nemeth. "Yes. But it's not the outward appearance that's the scary part, it's just how easily we were able to extrapolate his personality from the cloud. The robot doesn't just *look* like the Crown Prince, it has access to his full personality banks since birth, all of his cloud-linked memories…it's entirely possible that one day-"

Tilda spoke the words before Nemeth could. "It could replace him?"

Nemeth nodded sadly. "He doesn't see the danger. But in a regime like this, where he's already rubbing certain people the wrong way with his liberal reforms-"

"Jävla fan!" Tilda cursed.

"Indeed." agreed Nemeth, taking a drink.

Tilda glanced around, frowned and lowered her voice to a whisper, no longer sure that this was a wise venue for such a conversation. Nemeth, in his drunken stupor was being reckless. Still, she had to know.

"You mentioned that two such replicants exist. If the Crown Prince has one, may I know who has the other?"

Nemeth put down the claw and looked at her sadly.

"Me." He answered sullenly.

Tilda understood everything now. Nevertheless, Nemeth decided he'd better explain. The aquatic ambience of the Al Mahara now taking on the atmosphere of a church confessional booth.

"I couldn't countenance greenlighting the project without testing it on myself. It's why I ultimately gave up on my principles and went all-in on cloud connection. The first replicant is a carbon copy of me. We've never let it out of the lab. I won't allow it…but still…" he paused.

"You're afraid of it."

Nemeth smiled. "You're probably thinking that *this* is the big secret I talked about …but it's not that. It's something much simpler." And he raised a finger, tapping the tiny pin badge of a space rocket that sat fastened to his lapel.

Tilda had noticed it already, way back on the roof, considering it a poor match for the expensive suit it adorned, dismissing it as the eccentricity of a billionaire.

"My father gave this to me." Nemeth explained "It's all I have of him. A secret that I keep to myself. In fact, you're the only person I've ever explained it to. I don't know why that is. I guess…" he narrowed his eyes "I guess I'm testing you. I want to see if you really can keep a secret because, one day…I might need you to tell someone."

"I don't understand." said Tilda.

"Ever since we made the replicant…the android version of myself. I've worn this badge at public events. I hadn't known what to do with it before, but it's taken on a kind of strange significance. It's evidence, you see. Proof that, unlike the replicant, I had a real past; I had a father. I'm not sure what will happen to us in the future, but I feel like increasingly, as these things become more commonplace, we might need a way to distinguish. To remember which things were really done by us, or which were the work of our clones. The android…He won't wear the badge. Nobody would ever pick this out for a man like Roger Nemeth; this small thing of tin and memories. So now you know…now you'll always know how to tell the real me from the fake." He winked at her, shook his head and signalled the waiter to bring over a fresh drink.

The Nemeth on the screen had not worn the badge.

Her calls and emails went unanswered over the coming weeks as she returned to Stockholm and watched the events play out from home.

The badge-less Nemeth was everywhere. Adverts, late night TV chat shows. Always the same Nemeth. Always without the badge.

She resigned from her position as editor at *Aftonbladet* and drove her daughter, Ebba, to their cabin in Lindvallen. The days of skiing had long since passed, but it was tolerable in what was still considered winter in Sweden. From there she made the formal applications to join the Scandinavian arks and, in the evenings, when Ebba was tucked up in bed, she powered on her keyboard and worked on the bombshell article she hoped to leave as a parting gift to the people of America.

One morning, not long after finishing the article, she received a small parcel in the mail. She was surprised by its arrival as she had told no one about her plans to move there. When she tore open the brown wrapping paper, she found a tiny, jewellery box inside. She opened it and almost dropped it when she saw what was inside.

The tiny, worn enamel pin badge of a rocket lay offset against the black velvet case.

Her first thought was that it was his apology, the official abdication of his dream. Then a quiet dread crept over her like the morning fog covering the lake as she realised the true nature of the message.

The parcel had not come from Nemeth.

There *was* no Nemeth anymore.

Only them.

Those shadowy forces who had first pretended to give countenance to his plans, then privately denounced them, rejected them and made their move to ensure that the next time 'Roger Nemeth' was seen in person, he was a bird singing a different tune.

She sat in the armchair on the veranda, overlooking the lake where the hated sun was rising, realising the futility of her situation, imagining the scenario as it would play out should her exposé hit.

She saw an image of herself sleeping in her room as shadowy figures, armed with a lifetime of private cloud-stored experiences and other more dangerous things, entered her cabin. She saw Ebba waking up the next morning and walking, sleepy-eyed into the kitchen calling for Mama and finding, instead, something else. A thing that looked and acted like Mama but was somehow, unexplainably… different.

Her hand swiped across the air and the virtual desktop flickered into life. With a trembling finger she selected the article she had been working on for weeks. It took all of her effort to delete it and even more not to scream as she did so.

She swiped away the screen then picked up the APD, wandered over to the lake and tossed it into the warm crystal waters where it sunk without trace to nestle among the silent, empty crayfish cages.

Collapsing back down in the chair, she picked up the little pin badge; all that remained of Nemeth now, and held it tightly in her fist, absorbing the pain of the metal as it cut into her palm. The tears fell from her cheeks as her eyes filtered up toward the clear and empty morning sky where the burning orange sun rose over the mountains, looking down on her like a single all-seeing eye.

*Michael Teasdale is an English author living in Cluj-Napoca, Romania. His stories have appeared in Shoreline of Infinity, Litro, Novel Magazine and The Periodical, Forlorn. He can also be found in anthologies by Havok Publishing, World Weaver Press and Tyche Books with audio adaptations via 'Havok Story Podcast' and 'The Other Stories'. He can be followed on X/Twitter @MTeasdalewriter*

# WYLD FLASH—FREE FICTION
# EVERY FORTNIGHT

## WWW.WYLDBLOOD.COM

# Oak and Ash

*Kate Kelly*

The forest fascinates me. I walk between the twisted trees. I should be meeting Sally. I'm late.

Years past someone left a bicycle propped against an oak. In time the tree grew round it, entombing it. These days it happens faster. A park bench, swelling bark pushing between the slats. A skate park, now root cracked concrete.

Something moves up ahead. Sally? I hasten to where we should meet.

No! You must never fall asleep with your back against a tree! I arrive in time to see the bark shift around her and the light go out of her eyes!

# Moon Dog
## R.L. Raymond

It has been three suns since the Man went away. That was when the meat-rot and fire-smoke stank up the inside of the house, seeping under the covers and blankets the Woman had stuffed against the windows and doors. His eyes were wet, his face sunken, his skin wounded. He managed to whisper *I love you* to the Woman, and, patting me on the head but never looking directly at me, added *I'll look for help.* Her eyes, also wet, didn't twinkle as they usually did. Without kissing her goodbye, he opened the door a crack, slid out and slammed it shut. I couldn't see anything outside. She shoved the rug back into place and cried.

I don't go in the backyard anymore. I long for the little patch of dry, prickly grass and the aromatic cedars lining the tall fences. But when the meat-rot smell blew in, they never let me out again. We didn't even go for walks. As embarrassing as it is, I have to relieve myself on word-paper tossed on the floor of a little closet we don't use. And with the Man gone, the Woman doesn't clean it up anymore. At first she did, and she had talked to me, pretending things would be ok, giving me the last of the treats. But after one sun passed, she stopped, busy instead watching the noise-box, listening to the man- and woman-heads yammer on about sickness and dying and burning.

She ignores me now, having left the giant bag of food knocked over on the kitchen floor beside a big dish of water. No matter how much I scratch or whine or bark, she doesn't respond. I don't seem to exist anymore.

When I relieve myself somewhere else in the house–I can't stomach my own stench in that closet–I stand up on my hind legs and peer out any window I can. It's difficult to see with the bunched-up fabric everywhere. I can see a few men and women, some big, some small, lying down, on the lawns, in the street, not moving. I see the other neighbourhood dogs wandering by themselves, a few licking bodies, one of them chewing and gnawing. I have to turn away. At another window I see a cat, sneaking around, avoiding the dogs and the bodies, looking for birds to chase. But the sneaky cat looks different, scared. Far away, in the sky, I see fire-smoke mix with the clouds.

#

The noise-box stops working early after the fourth sun. The Woman paces back and forth, hacking and coughing, and then she slams the set, punching at it. Maybe I can cheer her up. But when I approach, tail wagging, eyes as kind as I can muster, she turns on me. This Woman who never as much as raised her voice starts howling, gargling ugly, wordless sounds from her distorted, patchy, darkened face. And she grabs a glass and throws it in my direction. It misses, but I am not safe anymore. I growl, backing away. I don't want to hurt her. She picks up the sweep-broom and lunges at me, holding it over her head. I don't want to bite her. She brings it down and I duck, slipping past. She loses her footing and falls, dropping the weapon. We are face to face. Liquids drip from her mouth and nose. Heat emanates from her. She smells wrong. I ready myself to attack. This isn't the Woman I know. She is different, frightened and frightening. I would be doing her a favour, sinking my teeth into her throat. But before I can decide, she croaks *I'm sorry*, drags herself to her knees, to her feet, wobbles, and walks to the door, kicking the carpet away, and she opens it, racing off into the grey.

I've never been outside in the front without that uncomfortable strap around my neck. Whenever the Man or the Woman took me for a walk, they would lead me, drag me, but always pull me away from bad things. I hated it, but I understood. They saved me from a few nips and more than one encounter with a car. Now there is nothing to pull me back from the dangers out here.

The stench is gut wrenching. I bring up the last of my food right there on the top step. As much as I want to leave the house to find the Woman and the Man, I am scared. There are more bodies than I thought, and the dogs are all over. Some are sitting quietly beside stinking corpses, others run around without purpose, and across the way, one is muzzle deep in a man's guts, face slick and dark with blood, baying at the black birds swooping down for their share. It's not a house dog–it's one of the coyotes the Woman always worried about

when we walked closer to nightfall. I notice another dog yelping and looking at me. We know each other, our Women often walking together and giving us enough slack to sniff and pick up sticks. I bark back and it runs over to me.

-This isn't good.

-No.

-Looks like all the men and women.

-Mine just ran.

-Yeah, I saw her. She won't last long.

-How do you know.

-Two moons ago my Man ran out. Didn't come back. Look around.

-I'm scared.

-We're all scared.

-Where's the fire?

-Coming this way. In cars.

We decide to stay together. Now brave enough to step out, I follow it along, trotting at a good pace, taking in as much as I can, trying to figure out what to do next.

-My Man and Woman are gone for good aren't they?

-That's a given. They're all gone from what I can tell. Except for the glass-faces.

-Glass-faces?

-Yeah. They're the ones bringing the fire.

We run fast, the death-waft filling our snouts. There is not a single person to be seen alive. We cut through yards where, in the past, we would have been yelled at for relieving ourselves against a tree. Now, there is only barking, and songbirds, the occasional cat, squirrels, and racoons in trees, on roofs, each as mystified as the last. And there are no mechanical sounds: no rolling cars, no buses, no sirens, no bicycles. We press on, harder, unable to escape the wafts of what now smell more of meat and wood and chemicals.

-Ok slow down. Let's be careful. They're over there.

We are hidden behind a hedge, looking down the road into a neighbourhood I don't recognize. I have never been this far. The heat is fierce and the smell almost chewable: men in strange, thick clothing with glass over their faces stand beside large, cube-cars holding a type of vacuum cleaner that I've seen my Woman use in the past. Their faces are invisible behind the reflection of the corpses piled up and the blazes dotting the pavement. They form a line and walk slowly. When I expect them to turn on their cleaners, I nearly choke. They are spitting fire! Flames burst out, torching the bodies, all the animals that had come for a closer look scattering. The glass-faces move along, burning every body they come across. We crouch low. There is a commotion at one of the houses, and a little woman walks through a glass door, without appearing to notice. Immediately, one of the men turns a fire-spitter in her direction and ignites her, bathing her in flame until she melts on herself, smouldering. When the glass-face turns away, we hear a deep, low growl come from the same house. Running past the charred, bubbling mass, a large, muscular dog charges the killer. It stops short, circling, enraged.

-He's going to kill it!

-Keep quiet…

I can't watch the poor mutt get doused in fire. Luckily, it doesn't happen. Mad, the dog leaps, three or four body lengths and clamps down on the thick-suited arm. It falls back to the ground with a large chunk of material hanging from its teeth. Before the dog has a chance for a second round, another glass-face intervenes, raising the fire-spitter, but spraying the man with the damaged arm. Bewildered, the dog spits out the wad and backs away, barking at the blazing form twisting and dancing before him. When the man stops, crumpled and blackened, the mutt runs away from the chaos.

-They don't care no matter what we do. It's like we don't exist.

-Down, they're on the move…

The glass-faces, including the man who killed the other, gather at the end of the street, turn around, focus on the houses. Walking between the meat-fires, they march up each driveway, kick open doors, break windows, and spew flames inside. Instantly the houses glow brightly, and smoke grows heavier.

-That's why we can't go back home.

-What do we do now?

-We go farther.

All the dogs tell us the same story: all the humans are dead, except for the glass-faces, and all the houses are burned. Oddly enough, not one of them remembers seeing one dead animal. We walk the whole day, going farther, and by the time the sun is sinking in the sky, there are many of us, including cats that took the time to communicate with us. They were hard to understand at first, with their mews and meows, but we've managed, with a few wags and flicks, especially helped by a pair, a dog and a cat that lived together now reunited.

Not knowing what lies ahead brings us together, or maybe fear, or instinct. Whatever the case, we are now a considerable group. There are even wild animals in our ranks. We can't understand them, but there is an agreement, a peace that settles over us. We promise the mice and squirrels and doves and robins that we will not harm them or chase them or eat them. The coyotes keep their distance, but I am certain they too wish to abide by the rules, at least for the time being.

We travel farther, but the smell of meat- and wood-smoke lingers. We have long left the neighbourhoods, cutting into the fields where more critters pad alongside us. It doesn't matter that only humans are dead–we are all lost, confused, afraid. One of the cats who darted off earlier comes back at full speed. It gestures and does its best and we soon come to understand that it has spotted another group, bigger than ours, nearby on a hilltop. They too, for now, appear accepting and kind. We walk farther and join them.

We've travelled as far as we can. The sun has set. We stand at the summit, in our hundreds, watching the bright fires burn in every direction. We have all lost something this day. Each one of us has seen a little piece of the world end. How we survive from now on, how we react to one another, we can only guess. I am sure of one thing: I've grown accustomed to the smell of meat-smoke. I barely notice it anymore. Now it is just smoke, filling the sky, thick and dark, making it difficult to see the newly risen moon.

*An Imagist, R L Raymond tells stories through fiction, poetry, and photography. He earned his Master of Arts in English Literature from the University of Western Ontario and has been published around the world in journals and hallways, on a bus and a few postcards. Please visit www.RLRaymond.com for more information.*

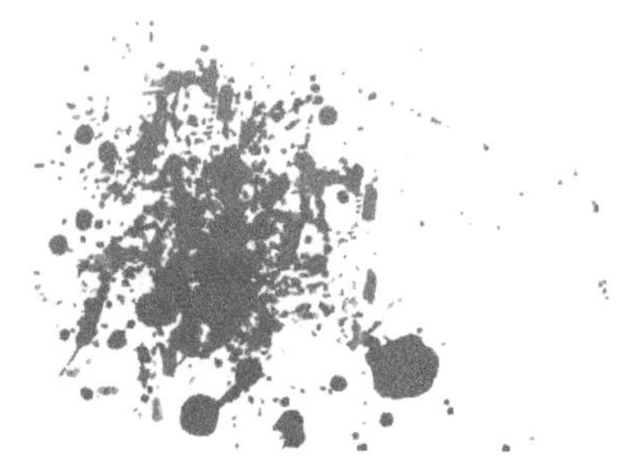

# From Airlock to Eternity

*Addison Smith*

I drift away from the Pegasus, the ship becoming little more than a beacon in my vision pulsing red above the atmosphere. I slow my breathing as the cold surrounds me, and for a moment I know peace.

The infection burns in my blood and hungers to spread, infect, devour. My body fights but cannot win. I will die with blessed quickness as my vision blurs and is lost to the darkest depths.

A voice whispers through my headset: "Pegasus, you're cleared for landing."

I grin and my lips crack and bleed. I release it. And now it will feed.

*Addison Smith is an author and laborer living in upstate New York. His fiction can be found in Fantasy Magazine, Fireside Magazine, Daily Science Fiction and others. He has recently discovered the joys of brewing coffee in numerous ways, and will gladly talk your ear off @AddisonCSmith*

# Litter

*Tiffani Angus*

The dogs herded the boys together. Three sharp whistles came out of the air and the dogs stopped, waiting, their tails curled like question marks.

Quint ordered the younger boys to stand with their backs against the red wagon and hold up their weapons. The day before, he'd collected a few thin sticks along the side of the path and sharpened them with a small kitchen knife, using what he could remember reading in the *Boys' Adventure Series*. He'd armed every last boy, down to Sec and Lem, the youngest. But what little moonlight that leaked through the brown haze barely allowed the children to see well enough to defend themselves. Yet it was the sounds, which none of the boys had ever heard before outside of videos—no animals were allowed inside the Facility—that scared Quint the most. He tried to follow their whistling and whining, but his weak flashlight couldn't keep up as they circled the camp, pushing the boys together into an ever smaller clump.

Sec whimpered from the other side of the wagon. A growl rolled through the darkness, giving Quint the chance he needed. He lunged and felt his spear crack against a solid body.

Two short whistles and the boys were left alone.

"Is everyone here?" Quint whispered.

"Me and Lem," Sec answered.

"Talley?" Quint asked. Talley answered, and then on down the line each boy's voice, a lone mouse of sound small and scared, came through the dark. "Sec and Talley, you two keep watch for a while. Then wake me and Wal. It's better to be in twos."

The next morning, Sec's screams woke the camp. "Lem! LEM!" He drew out the small name until it grew to fill the desert valley. No answer came from his littermate.

Quint counted. It was one of the things he did best, after reading. One wagon, seven boys, eight blankets, one path. He came back to the boys and the blankets again, but this time didn't count himself. Six boys, their hair the color of the dust that had settled over them as they slept. Seven blankets, once blue but now just as brown and gritty as the bodies they covered each night.

Lem was missing. Lem with eyes the color of the garden in the courtyard where the boys had played every afternoon. Lem called *pup* because he was smallest. Lem who'd never been beyond the Facility's outer walls in his short six years. Not until the lights went out and the locks unlocked forever and the doors opened and those who were left walked out of the corridors of glass and metal and into the shadows of the brown-grey mountains.

Yesterday Quint was one of eight. *Oct.* Dr. Boone had taught him that. Dr. Boone had taught him nearly everything. How to count, how to take away, how to read. Enough knowledge for one of the younger boys, but not what Quint really wanted to know, like how to find water, where to find food, what was at the river, and why a boy disappeared in the night. And the most important lesson of all, the one that Quint had not found in any book: how to find a Mother.

A whistle far off carried on the wind. Shading his eyes with one hand, Quint searched the blurry horizon. Talley said "Dogs" and began to cry. Quint was almost glad of the distraction from his hunger, but the danger of the animals was still fresh in his mind. He'd had to use all of his power as the oldest to keep the boys from running toward the dogs when they'd first spotted the animals days before. They recognized the furry bellies and perky ears, wagging tails and toothy smiles from picture books, and wanted to romp and play. But Quint had read a book about a dog that had gone bad, had turned into a wolf and eaten people. The little ones had to listen to him. He knew things.

Lem's pack, a small khaki duffel bag rummaged from a forgotten supply closet deep in the Facility, lay camouflaged against the dirt. Inside Quint found three mostly empty water bottles, a half-full baggie of dried fruit and nuts, and a squirrel's nest of colors: Dr. Boone's name badge with a red symbol like a twisted ladder around a lower-case *t*; three plastic spoons (yellow, green, and pink); a purple crayon from the arts-and-crafts room; a few snippets of yarn; and a folded drawing of several stick figures, their names printed in thick black marker (Lem and Sec, Talley and Wal, Quint and one of his brothers, Rom). At the end of the line of boys, drawn as tall as the paper would allow, stood Dr. Boone, gone and left behind now in the buildings sunk below the earth.

Quint stored the water and food in his own pack, added the spoons to a pile on the wagon, pocketed the crayon, and half buried the rest by shoving it into the dirt beneath a scrub brush. Fewer boys meant more for those left. Quint had quickly learned the mathematics of survival.

He handed the duffel to Sec to replace the boy's disintegrating paper bag. "Put your stuff in here."

"Are we going to look for him?" Sec asked, his eyes narrow in his sunburned face. "Maybe he went back," he offered. "Lem could be home, with Dr. Boone and the others."

"They're all dead, Sec. Or gone. We can't go back." Quint pointed in the direction they were headed. "It's important to find the river."

"Lem's important."

"Lem's gone, Sec. We're running out of food and water. We have to find the river like Dr. Boone said."

Sec toyed with a hole in his shirt before he asked in a whisper so low that Quint almost couldn't hear him, "Did Lem take any food?"

"When Lem gets hungry, he'll follow the path back to us. Let's go now."

A few hours down the trail and the sun hung halfway up in the sky where it throbbed in the haze. With the sky and land a blend of color, picking out rocky outcroppings and calculating distance took practice. A week out of the Facility and Quint still found it difficult to understand the size and emptiness of the world.

*The river,* Dr. Boone had said. *It's east.* Concrete corridors with arrows and small windowless rooms dulled whatever sense of direction Quint might have learned naturally. He was left to consult a scratched old compass and the map, folded so many times that it had lost all color along the folds, leaving him to guess what was between him and the blue line of river along its far right edge. They were probably still far from the river, he guessed. In the *Boys' Adventure Series,* the land along a river was green with grass and trees.

Before he'd got too weak to speak, Dr. Boone had shown Quint how to read the map key and how to use his little finger to measure the miles. When Quint had asked how far a mile was, Dr. Boone had just shut his eyes.

The boys walked single-file ahead of him along a dirt path curved around the base of a hill. While he pulled the wagon handle with one hand, Quint scratched the crayon in his pocket with the other and stared in wonder at the purple half-moons under his nails. They stopped for a break when their weak shadows nearly disappeared under their feet. Wal and Talley—quick with curly hair, likely littermates—scrutinized Quint's movements as the oldest boy rationed out what little food was left. If they were careful, they might have enough to last the rest of the day and partway into the next. He only allowed each a small sip of water, worried that it wouldn't last as long.

Quint sat against the wagon in his usual spot. Sec, sitting furthest away, picked at his share of food. "Show us the cut-outs," Quint said, hoping to bring the boy back into the group. In the stories, children taken in the night usually didn't return unless they were particularly strong or smart, and Lem had been neither.

Sec ignored the order until the other boys took up the chorus. "Pictures! Show us the pictures, Sec. Please!"

Most had been cut from the magazines stored in the arts-and-crafts room. A few were photographs that Sec had stolen from desk drawers and the Facility's private quarters after all but Dr. Boone had left and the systems had failed.

They were all of Mothers. Smiling in clothes the colors of flowers and holding babies. Walking as they pushed babies in special carts. Sitting in a shiny machine under a bright awning that said "Texaco," a man leaning in a window with a rag in his hand and two children smiling from their seats behind her. Leaning over to kiss a small child in a dark bedroom, a tiny light glowing in the corner. "Mothers," Sec whispered.

"Where's the one with the food?" Talley asked.

At the mention of food, everyone moved closer to look. Sec carefully laid down the cut-out of the Mother surrounded by platters of vegetables and fruits, some never grown in the Facility's gardens. They knew from asking Dr. Boone that the large brown item she carried on a tray was a turkey, and Quint wondered for the hundredth time what it might have tasted like. The doctor had described it as close to chicken, but Quint was sure that nothing so round and heavy could be as bland as their usual Wednesday-night meal.

He watched as Sec considered each boy before trusting him with a cut-out or a photograph. But there was one photo he'd only ever let Quint touch: Dr. Boone, much younger but still him with dark hair and glasses, his face smooth and naked, sitting on a couch with an older Mother. They had the same nose and lips, her face a mirror of his but with a softer chin. On the back, written in smudged blue ink: *Mom & Bradley, 1998.* Quint knew from the calendar on Dr. Boone's desk that the photo had been taken nearly fifty years before, and he could not imagine ever being that old.

Wal asked Sec to tell the Mother story. Usually the boys waited until it was time to sleep to ask. As Sec began, Talley pointed to a puff of dust floating at the edge of the track where it curved around the hill.

"Look!"

The figure that walked out of the cloud was even dirtier than them. Ripped pants and a ragged-edged coat flapped around grimy ankles. A grubby cloth and slouched hat hid the eyes and face.

A high, scratchy voice called out, "Hi."

The figure strode up to the boys, hands on hips, and the truth was exposed in the hills and valleys of her body, so different from anyone who walked the halls of the underground world they had once called home. "My name is Fynn."

They had never seen a woman. Not in the Facility. Not carrying turkeys or driving vehicles or holding babies or kissing the heads of little golden-haired boys as they drifted off to sleep. Quint, like most of the boys, dreamed of Mothers. Among the youngest it was a kind of currency traded for favours: the dreams of the cut-outs come to life, of aprons and smartly tied scarves, pink frosted cakes and hugs before breakfast. This sharing usually led to speculation about how a Mother smelled after cooking dinner or how her skin might feel or the sound of her voice.

Quint's shock turned to disappointment that she didn't have shiny hair and a gentle smile, a dress that puffed up around her knees, or at least a flowered scarf tied neatly around her neck rather than an odd pair of goggles with inky black lenses.

The realization of what she was buzzed through the band of boys like static electricity.

They stared at Fynn, whose name they would later say just to see her turn her head and look at them, but never with the look of satisfaction at a job well done like the Mother busy mopping around the baby in a highchair. The wind rattled the photograph Sec still held in his hand.

Quint stepped forward. She was taller than he, which was as it should be with a Mother, he decided. "Where did you come from?"

The wind snaked up beneath the cloth, lifting it to expose Fynn's mouth and twisted lips, as she laughed. The smallest boys flinched at the sound that was so similar to the yelps and barks of the dogs in the night.

She patted her belt and Quint recognized what she had as a gun, and he wanted to feel its weight in his hand. She pointed toward the path and the hill that it curved behind. "Thought I'd see if I could get a dog. Cats are too scarce: too small, too, to sell or trade for much. But, really, any meat is good."

"Hey?" Sec called to Fynn with a quick sideways glance at Quint, who was about to ask what she meant. "Lem's gone. Did you see him?"

Quint grabbed the boy's thin arm.

"Lem your dog or your Dad?" Fynn asked. She studied Sec, studied his face and measured him.

"No, he was my littermate. He got lost. A real Mother would help us find him."

"Don't listen to him," Quint said. Before Sec could interrupt, Quint asked again, "Where are you from?"

She tipped her head back and the cloth around her mouth lifted again, but what she said made Quint forget to ask about the scars. "Warren. Near the river."

"This river?" He pulled the map back out of his pocket and thrust it at her.

Fynn glanced down but didn't take the map. She pointed at the wagon piled high with blankets and packs. "I haven't eaten in a while. Got anything?"

None of the books or pictures had taught Quint what to do when a Mother asked for food, so he motioned to the wagon and let her take what she wanted. She could find more and they would all be full and the little boys wouldn't cry and whine anymore that they were hungry.

Fynn shoved food up under the wrap covering her face, but the wind flapped the cloth around and got in her way. So with one quick look at Quint she pulled it down around her neck. He stared at the puckered red skin that ran from her nose, over her lips, and down under her chin.

"Why don't any of you have the scars?" she asked around a mouthful of stale bread and dried fruit. The little food they had left was disappearing at an alarming rate.

Quint shrugged. "Should we? I've got this, though, from when I burned myself." He rolled up a crusted sleeve and pointed to a white scar along the inside of his wrist. "I wanted to help the cook. After that, Dr. Boone told us no more kitchen."

She studied it. "Huh."

He held it closer to her face, close enough to feel the breath from her lips and nose. But she didn't kiss it better like in the cut-outs.

"This doctor guy your father?"

He shook his head. "He said he was and he wasn't. But he's dead now, so I suppose I don't have one."

"Me either. Mother's gone, too," Fynn added. "Not many grown-ups left, really. But I can take care of myself."

Quint's chest hurt when she said it. *Mother.* She'd had one. He'd never thought of Mothers having Mothers. "Where did yours go?"

Fynn shook her head in small movements while she chewed. "Where everyone else went when the cloud came."

Quint didn't have a chance to ask more before she stood and strode off the edge of the path. "Coming?" she called back over her shoulder.

The other boys got up to follow. Fynn shook her head and pointed at Quint. "Just you."

As they walked, he offered his knowledge of the dogs. Fynn nodded as she skidded down into small gullies and climbed over outcroppings until the boys and wagon blended into the landscape behind them.

"Where are you all from?" Fynn asked.

Quint remembered Dr. Boone saying that the Facility kept them all safe, especially after what he called The Storm. Dr. Jenkins argued with Dr. Boone and left, only to come back a few days later, skinny and wide-eyed, his nostrils and lips red and raw. After Dr. Jenkins died, Dr. Boone lectured the boys. "You were all born here. You belong here, inside with me. It's the only safe place for now." And it had been, until Dr. Boone had stopped eating and had started teaching Quint about maps and rivers and towns.

"That way." Quint pointed back along the way they had come.

"I know that," Fynn said. "But why do you all look alike? Why are you all together?"

Quint picked at the purple crayon wax beneath his nails. "Some of us are littermates—brothers. We all lived together at a place for boys." He could not bring himself to tell her. He felt as if she should just know.

"Like an orphanage?"

He felt his skin heat up where she looked at him.

She misunderstood and explained. "It's a place where kids with no parents live."

"I know that," Quint said. "We were all born there."

She was silent but looked like he did when he was adding or taking away. She was calculating.

"So what's at the river that's so important?" she asked.

"Don't you know?"

Without a sound, Fynn pulled the gun from her hip and pointed it at Quint. None of the pictures had shown a Mother with a gun.

"Come out," she said. Behind Quint, stones rattled and Sec appeared.

The young boy strode out without any fear. "Dr. Boone would say you're nosy," Sec said.

She whistled. "My Mom would say you're mouthy. But yeah, I'm curious. It's the only way to know what's what."

Barking diverted Sec's attention. In the vista below them, the air wavered and shifted, and Quint picked out the dogs, darker brown than the land around them, loping down the path toward the boys. He was leaning across the rock to yell and warn the others when the world cracked open and the air in the valley concussed in his ear.

The *Boys' Adventure Series* didn't prepare him for the sound or the smell of a gun being fired. His ears rang with it as he followed Fynn back down the hill and across the valley to where the others stood waiting. She had missed.

Sec picked up his stick and waved it in the directions the dogs had run. "We have to follow them to find Lem."

"They won't be back around, at least not for a while," Fynn explained.

"Why won't anyone look for Lem?"

Fynn ignored him and sent the other boys to collect whatever they could find that would burn. In the week they had been on the path there had been no fire: another thing Quint hadn't learned. Now thanks to Fynn's lighter, they had warmth and light in the night.

Sec and Quint sat on opposite sides of the fire. The other boys sat near Fynn and snuck hungry glances at her, their eyes wetly flashing in the firelight. She told stories about going to school and eating in restaurants. No one asked to see the pictures.

Quint took up his spear and shoved the knife into this belt before taking the first watch.

Later, he pretended to sleep and forced himself to stay still while Fynn's presence glowed like a second fire, small boys drawn to her side like moths to light. He lay awake long into the night, listening to the tiny shifting movements of a Mother in the darkness.

The next morning, Quint woke to find everyone but Fynn still asleep, even the watch. He counted. Six boys, six blankets.

"He's gone," she said.

"The dogs?" he asked. She shrugged.

Sec wasn't lost. There was no grey duffel, no cut-outs of Mothers, no photograph of a younger Dr. Boone.

Fynn stood in the center of the group. "You still want to go to the river?"

Quint nodded.

"Well, follow me then."

They woke the boys and she started walking, her back straight, her coat swaying around her like a skirt.

Bellies beyond empty, the boys followed her along the path and around the hill. Quint remembered pictures of cities and towns and villages. The Facility's buildings, white and clean, had hugged low to the ground and disappeared into the hard desert floor. But these structures stood without shame or fear, blatant in their size and shape.

A grey-brown dust covered everything, smothering color and line. The walked around and over broken glass, empty cans, bags, abandoned shoes, piles of cloth.

The busted Texaco sign, its fragile stalk holding a top-heavy flower, swayed above them. When the boys asked what these places were, she looked at them with eyes hard and flinty as the stones Talley liked to spit on and shine up then keep in his pockets.

Fynn pointed out buildings. "House, beauty shop, supermarket, gas station.

Gas stations don't matter anymore. No more cars. The markets and stores are all empty. Sometimes you can find a dented can under a shelf. The labels are gone and you don't know if you have peaches or corn. But food is food."

Quint read the words along the roof of a long building with several doorways and windows. Dentistry, Check Cashing, Laundromat, Cafe. He wished he knew what they meant but felt that asking would draw her dark gaze to him.

Fynn pushed open an empty door frame, its glass gone but for jagged teeth left around the edges. Footprints of different sizes danced and shuffled across the dirty floor, pulling Quint past benches with ripped-out stuffing, around the counter, and toward the refrigerators and cabinets that hung open, empty and cavernous as his stomach. He rejoined the others near the door. Talley picked up and dropped the handle from a broken mug.

"Fynn?" Wal held a large card out to her.

She rubbed the dust from the page and pointed to the photos of food, shiny and smooth. "This one was my favorite. Strawberry shake, fries, cheeseburger. What was yours?"

Quint remembered a story with three wishes that were granted—for riches, for beauty, for love—and thought of the Mother under the Texaco sign. He'd already been granted one desire. Food would be easy now. As Quint and the boys collected all the pictures they could find, Fynn ventured out of sight around the counter. A whistle soared and dived like the birds in the dull desert sky, terrifying with sharp beaks and claws.

A dog trotted into the room and toward the boys. Talley screamed and dropped the cards, scattering their wishes across the sandy floor.

Three men stood still and dark on the other side of the glassless windows with ropes and guns in their belts. Two were bare-faced with scars like Fynn's. The other wore a scarf wrapped from eyes to chin, sporting a muddy oval where Quint imagined his mouth to be.

"Fynn!" Quint called. She didn't answer but he heard her footsteps behind him.

Outside, beyond reach, their wagon and spears sat alone in the street. Quint pulled the knife from his pocket and one of the bare-faced men touched the gun at his side and said, "Drop it, sonny."

He remembered the crack of Fynn's gun as she tried for the dogs, and the knife slipped from his hand and thunked to the floor where it sent up a tiny puff of dust.

Quint found himself in a line with the boys, a head taller than the rest but not quite tall enough. Fynn whistled, low and sweet, and something soft and warm pushed against Quint's hand, and his fingers sunk into the fur of one dog while another pushed a wet snout against his leg. The whistle blew again, this time two short bursts, and the dogs slunk behind Fynn, through the door hole and out to the men.

"This all of them?" the man closest to Fynn asked, his voice low and hard with dust and grime.

She nodded and stepped back. "Yep. These six and the other two you got."

"They were part of this group?"

"Yeah, but one took off home and the other tried to follow," she said. "Dogs scared 'em, so it was easier to bring 'em myself."

He nodded. "They look good, too. Clean. No scars."

"Told you."

"Watch your mouth, little girl," he said. "That's yours." He tilted his head toward a box a few feet behind him. Fynn picked it up quickly and turned to leave.

Before Quint knew he was even going to say it, the sounds left his lips, a high note followed by a low. "Mother?"

She turned but kept her hand on the gun at her hip and shook her head. The same male voice chuckled and then coughed, and Quint shrunk in on himself.

As the men silently gathered the boys together, they studied the unmarked skin, pinched their arms, and checked their teeth. Fynn, the dogs at her heels, stepped up to Quint. He sniffed hard to clear his nose and rubbed a fist under one eye while waiting for her to speak, to tell him that everything would be all right, to smooth his hair with a delicate hand, to teach him the lessons he would need for what would happen next.

Her eyes never left his as she reached into her pocket, pulled out the folded photo, and offered it to him with scabbed and bloody fingers. The inscription on the back was barely legible, the loops and circles of *Bradley 1998* all that was left clear. "Here," was all she said.

He shoved it in his pocket before the men tied one hand to Talley, the other to Wal, and led them all back out into the street. The little boys sniffed and cried, but said nothing.

Quint could not help but watch Fynn as he was dragged away.

"Where are we going?" he asked her.

"The river. I told you I'd get you there." She pointed down the street. He didn't know how he'd missed it: a dull blue-gray stretch, sunlight sparking on its surface.

"And then what?"

She shrugged. "Dunno."

One of the men laughed, low down in his throat. "That's because no one wanted a girl with a melted face."

Quint caught Fynn try to hide the wince, but the man saw it and laughed at her again. She reached for her gun, but he grabbed her arm and bent it behind her.

"I don't mind that mouth, little girl," he said in her ear. Fynn struggled but the man held her close with little effort. "But you stink," he said finally before pushing her to the ground and stepping away. There was something in the way she lay in the dirt, her arms tight at her sides, that reminded Quint of Dr. Boone's body, thin and ragged, a mar in the clean white Facility where they'd left him in his bed.

Fynn got to her feet. She lifted a hand, and he expected her to wave like the Mother standing in the doorway while her children walk along a green lawn with books in their arms. Instead she pulled the cloth up over her face and then whistled for the dogs, picked up her package, and hurried away through the dust and down the empty street.

And for the first time in his life, Quint knew homesickness. He was done with the *Boys' Adventure Series*, done with being in charge, done with counting and calculating.

"Move," the man said, and Quint was pulled along toward the river, the reflections on its surface the only clean thing in the world.

---

*Tiffani Angus, PhD, is the awards-shortlisted novelist of Threading the Labyrinth and short story author in several genres including fantasy, science fiction, horror, and even erotica. She's also the co-author of the writing guide Spec Fic for Newbies. She is currently a freelance writer, editor, proofreader, and educator.*

# Afterwards

*Kate Kelly*

It's been ten years – ten years since the world fell apart. I join you on the crest of the hill, a bottle of home brewed wine and two glasses. I pour.

Up here the world looks at peace, forest stretching away. I ventured into the city at first, after anarchy broke out, but soon retreated back to the mountain, back to you. Safe here as the world decayed. For a time.

I raise my glass.

"A toast," I say "to being the last humans on Earth."

I drink and pour yours onto your grave.

Ten years since you left me.

---

*Kate Kelly has had a number of short stories published in various SF magazines and anthologies and her children's novel, Red Rock, a Cli-Fi thriller for the 10+ age group was published by Curious Fox (an imprint of Raintree) in 2013 (UK). When not writing she works as a Marine Scientist.*

# The Dead Don't Lie
## Chris Cornetto

The corpse of Lord Theron, deceased a mere three days, hung pale and slack from the binding shackles.

Alenka knelt at the feet of the dead man, digging her nails into sweat-slick palms while the last witnesses shuffled into the sanctum. It had been a year since her last audience, a year of books and boredom in her cramped, lonely room, but the fear was still raw. She tried to recall her lines, to mentally recite the words the Divinus had given her, but terror crowded out all thoughts save one:

*The dead don't speak.*

Though she repeated the words like a mantra, willing them to be true, she couldn't keep her eyes from drifting to the serpent urn. The frieze-etched walls of the sanctum seemed to shrink, closing in to crush her. Suffocating wisps of incense writhed around her head. Her heart thudded in time with the drum, and together, they rose to a frenzy.

Two handlers, robed in black, prostrated themselves before the serpent urn. As one cautiously raised the lid, the other snatched with his tongs, quick as a snake himself. He had to be – though

dead, the asp inside was no less venomous. Or angry.

The Divinus thumped his staff, drawing the crowd's eyes away from the thrashing snake. He threw back his hood to reveal his shaved head and bony, angular face. "Friends and supplicants," he intoned, his voice as rich and smooth as lotus honey. "We are gathered to settle the matter of the Theron inheritance. We ask the aid of the dead, for the dead do not lie."

"The dead do not lie," echoed the crowd.

"The dead don't speak," Alenka whispered, but Lord Theron's blank stare and rictus grin mocked her denial. She fought not to look away.

"Lady Alenka Shan," the Divinus said, bowing before her. "Forty-first Deadspeaker. We beseech you to intercede on our behalf, to faithfully speak the words of the dead."

Despite her fear, Alenka found room for bitterness at the man's false deference. He knew better than anyone she was no Lady. He himself had 'discovered' her in the slums of Karakand, a city she barely recalled, and was fond of reminding her of her two qualifications for the role of Deadspeaker: a drug-addled mother who had sold her on the cheap, and her obedient participation in his mummer's show.

If only it *was* but a mummer's show. In a cruel jest of fate, Alenka feared she was far more qualified than the Divinus had ever guessed. *The dead don't speak,* she repeated, more wish than statement, as if wishing could make it true.

The Divinus nodded to the handlers, and with a flash of the ritual knife, the asps's severed head dropped to the floor. At once, inky blackness bubbled from the wound. It congealed into a cloud of spiraling vapor, which Alenka could swear was studying her – until the ring of torches flared to life, driving it back. The shadowy smoke retreated, vanishing into the corpse's mouth and nose as if inhaled.

The dead Lord Theron opened his eyes. And screamed.

Alenka clenched her teeth until her jaw ached, fighting the urge to shield her ears from the terrible, inhuman keening. She was the Deadspeaker. She had to listen, no matter how it split her head, how it stabbed at her brain until tears streamed down her cheeks.

The sound was awful, but worse, far worse, was the *understanding.*

*Hello, Alenka,* said the dead man. *I've missed you.*

Hearing that familiar, sibilant rasp, mingled with a baritone she assumed was Lord Theron's, the drumming in Alenka's chest missed a beat. When the Divinus had trained her, he'd assured her it would be mere noise – that he alone, and not the dead, would tell her what to say – but he was a liar or a fool. She licked her dry lips and forced them to form words.

"Departed spirit, forgive us who disturb your rest."

The corpse's shriek would have driven her to her knees, were she not already kneeling. And within that unholy sound, she heard the dead man's words.

*So formal. Is this not the third time we've spoken? Are we not yet friends?* The dead thing casually tested its bonds and found them secure. Its mouth flattened to a bare hint of a frown. *So little trust,* it lamented.

The third time, yet she'd never met Lord Theron? She'd had her suspicions, but it was a puzzle for later. She paused a moment to compose herself, reciting her next line mentally before attempting to speak it aloud. "Lord Theron, you were taken too soon, the matter of your heir undecided. We would know your will."

*Too soon? This swine? Never mind his heir – ask me of the singers, the cupbearer. Ask me where the stableboy's bones lie. Let us lay bare his secrets, and watch the fools blush in horror!*

Alenka's mouth moved like a fish gasping for air, but words had fled. The shrieking was bad enough. Why, *why* must it speak?

"Let the claimants step forth," the Divinus said for her. His glare of disapproval bored into her back.

Two women ascended the dais, one to each side of Alenka. The first, Kiara, was Theron's daughter, the only child of his first marriage. She looked to be in her late teens, like Alenka herself, and wore men's riding clothes. Her skin was dark from the sun, her boots caked in road-dust. The only indication of her status was a silver circlet that did little to tame her short, unruly hair. She wasn't pretty, per se, but faced the dead lord's unblinking eyes with fierce pride.

The other woman, barely older, looked a noble through and through. Gemma, Theron's second wife, was as fair-skinned and golden-haired as a fairytale princess. Her azure gown flowed from her curves like a cascade of water; her silver bangles flashed like waves catching the sun. Despite her haughty expression, she clutched her hands to hide their trembling.

*So this is the clever one,* Alenka thought. The matter was already settled in Gemma's favor, likely in exchange for a share of the Theron fortune. She cast Kiara a quick glance of pity. "My lord," she asked the corpse, "these women are known to you?"

The dead thing rattled its chains and screamed. Kiara flinched. Gemma clutched her ears and cowered.

*The brigand and the schemer? How dull. Let's discuss you.*

*Let's not,* Alenka thought. "Let the living plead their case," she declared, hoping to shift the dead man's attention.

Kiara seized the initiative, addressing the crowd with poise. "Though my father and I had been on poor terms for some years..."

Behind her, the corpse continued to howl, making it impossible for Alenka to concentrate. *Do you know how many Deadspeakers there have been?*

"...reconciled in secret, for fear of interference by his..."

*Three. Not forty-one. Just three, among a bevy of frauds.*

"...amended his will, in sight of Justice Morellen. But the Justice betrayed..."

*The second was younger than you when they burned her.*

"...this woman, who I will not call his wife, must have destroyed the will..."

*The Divinus himself lit the pyre, of course. He isn't one to be challenged by a girl with a gift.*

"...swear, and my father will attest, that I am his true and rightful heir."

Dead, cloudy eyes drifted past Alenka to the priest behind her. *What will he do, I wonder, when he learns of yours?*

The sweat of fear dripped down Alenka's brow, but she didn't dare wipe it. It stung her eyes, but she didn't dare rub them. In the dead Lord Theron's leering face, she could picture the skeletal grin of the Divinus as he held torch to her pyre...

A dusty riding boot nudged her, and Lord Theron's daughter shot her a glance of concern. It snapped Alenka back to her senses – enough, at least, to choke out the next line. "Will else of the living speak before the dead?"

Gemma stepped forth and cleared her throat, twisting a paper in trembling hands. By the pallor of her face, she looked half a corpse herself. "I... I..." she began, but the dead thing squawked, and she shrank back as if struck.

Alenka empathized, a little.

With a grunt of annoyance, the Divinus snatched the paper. "My lady, shall I read the statement on your behalf?" His expression made clear he was not asking.

The woman nodded, and slinked back to Alenka's side.

The Divinus smoothed the paper and held it before him – a gesture of pure theater, as he'd penned the notes himself. "I, Lady Gemma, rightful wife of Lord Theron..."

Again the shrieking crowded out Alenka's thoughts. *The dead don't lie, but that man does. Does it not gall you to lie for him?*

"...entire fortune to his infant son and only heir..."

*Hah. That babe is heir to naught but hay and horse dung.*

"...as attested by Lord Theron's spoken will, and by sacred right of primogeniture..."

*The poor girl, she truly believed the stableboy loved her. She was nothing to him but a means of revenge on her husband.*

"...with nothing set aside for the get of his first marriage, duly annulled..."

*She goaded Theron into killing the lad – an easy enough task, but not enough to hide her shame. Her belly swelled, and her husband was no fool.*

"...disgrace to her family, stripped of all inheritance..."

*Despite the lord's small regard for his daughter, he left her everything to spite the wife who dishonored him.*

"...all property due his son to be held in trust by his mother until he comes of age."

*Truly, what choice did the lady have but to poison her husband and burn his will?* The corpse's mouth twitched with a hint of amusement. *Such a tragedy.*

Alenka didn't want to believe the dead thing, didn't even want to hear it. It was none of her business; her duty was to say what she'd been told. But, try as she might, the words wouldn't come to her.

The Divinus gave an irritated cough. "The living have..." he hissed.

Thus prompted, the words wriggled off her tongue. "The living have spoken their peace. Let the dead now speak, and sort truth from lie like wheat from chaff. Honored departed, render upon us your sacred judgment."

The dead Lord Theron gazed at none but Alenka. He raised his chained arms to their fullest and let forth a soul-rending wail.

*My judgment? How quaint. I can see in the old man's greedy eyes what 'my judgment' will be.*

Alenka slumped forward, pressing her palms against the floor to keep from clapping them over her ears. She felt hot and dizzy and sick. If she had more nerve, if her legs had strength, she would run for the door – never mind that she'd be cut down in the attempt. Flight had long been an idle dream, but now it bubbled up more urgently than ever.

*Well, girl? Recite the words he gave you. Be partner in his lies.*

Though Alenka cared nothing for Lord Theron, she had no wish to cheat his heir. Kiara paid no mind to what others thought she should be. She was calm, confident, and fiercely herself – so opposite Alenka that she couldn't help but admire the girl. Yet how could Alenka defy the Divinus? Would he name her a fraud, and offer her to the flames? Behind her, the old priest growled his impatience.

*Speak,* goaded the corpse. *Speak, speak!*

"The honored Lord Theron has spoken," Alenka declared, reciting the words she'd committed to memory. The gods forgive her, what choice did she have? "The dead do not lie."

"The dead do not lie," echoed the crowd.

*Lie,* cried the corpse. *Lie, lie!*

Alenka tried to close her mind to the dead thing's words, but they beat against her thoughts like surf against sea cliff. "One clem..." She could feel the Divinus's glare as she stumbled over the words. She took a deep breath and began again. "One claimant has spoken truth before the dead. Let her be rewarded. One has spoken falsely." She told herself Kiara was a stranger, that she didn't owe the girl her life, but the words tasted no less foul on her tongue. "Let her be punished."

*Punished,* shouted the corpse, shaking its chains with glee. *Punished!*

"By Lord Theron's own word, spoken on this sacred altar, Lady Gemma is his true–"

*Murderer! Murderer!*

"...murderer."

Too late, Alenka clamped her hands over her mouth. The word that escaped was not the one she'd meant to say, but it could not be called back.

All fell silent, even the corpse. It leaned as close to Alenka as its chains allowed and stared with cloudy, dead eyes. Its face contorted, like slowly melting wax, into wicked grin of triumph.

What had she done? She gazed at the floor, willing it to swallow her. She'd betrayed herself, revealed her gift. Already, the heat of the torches felt like the first lick of the pyre.

"You lie!" shrieked Lady Gemma, shedding all grace and poise. "Harlot! Witch! You–"

"Silence!" Kiara barked, cutting off the woman's raving. "Did you think your treachery would fool the dead?" She knelt to help Alenka, who accepted the support gratefully, to her feet.

Gemma's mouth hung open. Her wide, blue eyes begged the Divinus for support, but he would not meet them. "The dead do not lie," he hissed through gritted teeth, shooting Alenka a glare that promised retribution. "End the ritual."

A handler, already in position, cranked the winch behind the altar, while the other stood ready with a heavy scimitar. The corpse of Lord Theron flailed and writhed against the chains as they drew inexorably taut. When it could struggle no more, it gave an ear-splitting wail of rage.

Alenka's knees went weak. She clutched her head, but hands could do nothing to quiet the voice booming through her mind.

*AGAIN TO MY PRISON! AND YOU, TO THE FLAMES! HEAR ME, GIRL – RELEASE ME, AND SAVE US BOTH! FREE M–*

The screaming ceased abruptly, followed by a dull thud. Through tear-blurred eyes, Alenka saw the handler with the sword step back from the altar. The other held in his tongs the corpse of another asp, ritually strangled. And on the floor, in a spreading pool of black ichor, Lord Theron's head gazed blankly past her.

Like bubbles of ink, black smoke issued from the corpse's neck. The shadow-thing darted about in a frenzy, but acolytes with torches closed in, corralling it toward the handler. With nowhere to flee, it escaped into the snake.

The dead asp thrashed, lunging suddenly for the handler. Its fangs snapped just short of his arm.

Only when the snake was secure in its urn, with the lid firmly shut, did Alenka realize Kiara was holding her up. Embarrassed, she eased her weight off the girl's shoulder. "Sorry," she mumbled.

Kiara gave her hand a reassuring squeeze. There were tears on her cheeks, too. "Don't apologize. Thank you for what you've done – for me, and for my father." She turned to the Divinus. "The matter is settled, then?"

"No!" cried Lady Gemma, clutching desperately at the priest's robe. "Our deal! You promised!"

"Remove her," said the Divinus, and two large acolytes gripped her arms while a third gagged her. The priest ground his teeth, staring at nothing, as they dragged her shrieking from the room. When she was gone, he thumped his staff and addressed the crowd gruffly. "The dead have spoken. Lady Kiara is Theron's true and only heir. Witnesses, you are dismissed."

As the crowd filed out, Alenka stood rooted in place, as fixed as the skeletons that adorned the temple pillars. She'd done right by Kiara, but the cost was too steep. The Divinus knew she could hear the dead. The thought filled her head with flames.

Flames licking at her feet. Flames gnawing up her legs. Flames devouring her whole.

She didn't even know she'd fainted until she woke with her head in Kiara's lap. The girl was arguing with the Divinus, but their words were hard to follow. Her head swam, and her ears felt stuffed with cotton.

"You forget," the girl said, "that I am now Lady Kiara Theron, not a child to be chased off with a broom. I will depart when I am ready."

The Divinus huffed. "Then stay as long as you please, but the Deadspeaker will return to her chamber." The click of his staff retreated from the sanctum.

Hooded acolytes closed in on all sides. Alenka wanted to cry out, but knew she'd get no sympathy from them. She didn't even know their names; she'd never been allowed to interact with the temple staff. Had it all been to keep them indifferent to her? To keep her disposable? She wriggled away from their grasping hands, but there was nowhere to flee.

"A moment, please!" Kiara swung an arm, waving the men back. She eyed Alenka with rising concern. "What troubles you, Deadspeaker?"

What was Alenka to say, and with the acolytes watching? That the Divinus had conspired with Lady Gemma to steal Kiara's inheritance? That she was a true Deadspeaker, and the Divinus a fraud? The truth would be nothing but fuel on the flames of her pyre. It touched her heart that Kiara had stood up for her, but the girl couldn't save her. No one could.

No one... except, perhaps, the dead.

*Release me*, the thing had said. *Release me, and save us both.*

Fragments of a plan shifted into place. Alenka pulled the girl close enough to whisper, close enough to breathe her scent of horses and meadow grass. There was nothing left but to gamble. "I have no right to ask this, but my life is in your hands. Can you be here, outside the temple, at midnight?"

Kiara eyed her gravely. She squeezed Alenka's hand and nodded.

Alenka paced her tiny room, her sanctuary and cage. An hour had gone by, then another, yet still the Divinus hadn't shown. She guessed it was nearing midnight. With effort, she pushed aside the thoughts of flames.

Three times now, she'd spoken to the dead thing. Despite what she'd been told, she was certain the shadow-smoke was more than theatrics – more, even, than a spell to animate the dead. It was an entity itself, some spirit or demon that wore corpses as if they were clothes.

No, it wasn't as simple as clothing. The creature took on aspects of its host. Its voice, even its personality, differed from body to body, and it couldn't speak at all in the skin of a snake. More, it knew what the dead knew – and, as far as she could tell, it did not lie.

Of course, honest wasn't the same as trustworthy. Though the shadow-thing had promised to aid her, she held no illusion it was her friend. How many years, she wondered idly, had it been prisoner in this temple? How many centuries a slave to the priests of the dead? She pitied the shadow-thing almost as much as she feared it. Her only leverage was that it hungered for release – but once free, then what? It wasn't a comforting line of thought.

A sudden knock cut her short, freezing her in her tracks. As she unconsciously smoothed her robe, her fingertips stung from nails chewed to the quick.

The door opened, and without awaiting permission, the Divinus stepped inside. He waved off the acolyte behind him, and ignored Alenka as the glow of the young man's lantern vanished around the corner. Quietly, the priest shut the door.

Alenka had intended to play meek, to plead ignorance, but her fists clenched of their own accord. She drew up straight and looked him in the eye.

But the Divinus only smirked at her defiance. "You disappointed me today," he said, his voice the soft, threatening hiss of a snake. Despite his outward calm, anger flashed in his coal-black eyes.

No matter her fear, Alenka was determined not to grovel. She remained silent, forcing him to speak.

"Nothing to say for yourself? Did you think there would be no consequences?"

Again she held her tongue. She'd never before had the spine to antagonize the Divinus, but by tomorrow, she'd be free or dead. The thought was liberating.

"Not only did you botch the verdict," he said, wagging an accusing finger, "somehow, you knew of Lord Theron's murder. That troubles me."

So, the Divinus knew Lady Gemma had killed her husband? And he conspired with her anyway? Somehow, Alenka wasn't surprised.

"Now who, I wonder, could have told you?" Despite the question, his smug tone made clear he'd already pieced it together.

She stared him down, offering nothing.

For a moment, a bare fraction of a second, he averted his eyes. "No excuse, then? No denial? I had expected you to at least protest your innocence."

The hypocrisy was more than Alenka could stand. "Innocence of what?" she snapped, bold with anger. If he'd

discovered her gift, why should she deny it? "I am the Deadspeaker! I spoke the truth of the dead, as told to me by the dead!"

To her surprise, the Divinus snorted as if she'd told a clever joke. "The truth of the dead, indeed? Last I saw, *Lady* Kiara was very much alive." His tone made a mockery of the honorific. "For now, at least…"

Alenka's mouth hung open, but she failed to form words. Had he still not realized she could speak with the dead? And what did Kiara have to do with this?

At Alenka's silence, the priest's thin lips stretched into a grin of wicked triumph. "Did you think no one would see you whispering with her?" He *tskd* in mock disappointment. "What did she offer? A share of her inheritance? Or something *more personal?*" He punctuated the question with a lascivious smirk. "Whatever the reason, you defiled the temple with her lies."

"No!" Alenka cried. She sank to her bed as strength drained from her legs. It was worse than she'd feared. The Divinus would brand her a heretic, and Kiara, too – all so he and Lady Gemma could steal Kiara's fortune. "That's not it at all!"

But the Divinus ignored her protest. *"Told by the dead,"* he chuckled, shaking his head. He opened the door, and from the hall outside offered a parting shot. "Sleep well, Deadspeaker. I promise to keep your trial brief."

The door thudded shut with the finality of a coffin lid. If she didn't escape tonight, she was doomed.

Shaking off her paralysis, Alenka reached under her bed and pulled free a thick wooden slat she'd worked loose earlier. She snuffed the oil lamp on her bureau, and placed an ear to the door while she waited for her eyes to adjust to the dark. Footsteps came and went in odd intervals. She thought she heard a soft snort, but it was hard to hear over the thudding of her heart.

It had always irked Alenka that her door had no lock, but today it was a blessing. She eased it open and peered cautiously into the hall. On a bench outside, an acolyte nodded in and out of sleep, a shuttered lantern at his feet.

Silently, Alenka thanked the gods for careless guards. Once certain they were alone, she tiptoed along the hall, her barefoot steps agonizingly slow. When at last she could reach the sleeping acolyte, she hefted the board – and brought it down with a *thud* on the back of his nodding head. She caught him as he slumped to the floor, careful to not upset the lantern. Pulse pounding in her ears, she glanced down the hall, waiting for someone to investigate the noise.

No one did. She eased her white-knuckled grip on the plank.

It was a matter of moments to drag the man to her room, strip his clothes, and bind and gag him in case he woke. She pulled low the hood of her new robe and made her way to the sanctum, the only exit she knew. From the shadows of the skeleton-carved pillars, four armed guards – double the usual number – glared at her. She fussed with the straps of her stolen sandals until the men lost interest, then ducked back into the hall.

Alenka had never been in the main wing of the temple. A wrong turn led her to a room where young acolytes sat up late playing knucklebones, but she slipped out before they noticed her. Another nodded as he passed her in the hall; she barely remembered to nod back. Tucked in her armpit, the wooden slat banged her shin with every step.

After a few zigs and zags, she came to a T-intersection, one path heading into darkness, the other well-lit. By instinct, she veered toward the darker corridor, but paused mid-step. Why, in the middle of the night, was a room lit so brightly?

Because the shadow-thing hated light.

Fearful someone might be watching, Alenka risked only a quick glance as she crept past the chamber. Not one, but a half-dozen serpent urns lined the wall, ringed by blazing sconces. Standing at attention, arms across his muscled chest, was the handler who'd cut off Lord Theron's head.

Alenka, heart thudding violently, pressed against the wall. She cursed herself for a fool. Of course the urn would be guarded. And why were there so many?

She peeked back in to see the handler cleaning his nails with the ritual knife. Cold despair crept down her spine. He was too alert to sneak past, too strong to fight – yet, unless she freed the shadow-thing, she was doomed to the pyre. She was dead either way.

Alenka gritted her teeth. Better a quick death than the flames.

She drew the plank from beneath her robe, and held it behind her back as she strolled into the room. The handler shot her a questioning look. She smiled back, and swung.

The man dodged the blow easily, but he hadn't been the target. It scythed through the air where his knees had been, and smashed into the nearest urn with an explosion of shattered crockery.

Inside, a dead snake.

"What are you doing?" the handler cried. "Are you mad?"

But Alenka didn't hesitate. With wild swings, she bashed urn after urn. It didn't matter who heard her now – all her hopes rested with the shadow-thing.

Two urns, three urns destroyed. More dead snakes.

As she swung for the fourth urn, a hand clamped around her wrist, halting the blow. She drove her elbow into the man's ribs, but his grip didn't ease. As he twisted her back, forcing her away from the remaining urns, she kicked and flailed at anything she could reach.

An urn teetered and fell.

The handler caught her around the neck and squeezed like a vise. Once, twice, he smacked her head into the wall, setting off explosions of pain and stars. He raised the ritual knife to her face – and froze, eyes wide with sudden recognition. "Deadspeaker? But why are you – *gah!*" His words cut off in a shriek.

Alenka dropped to the floor, and the knife clattered beside her. Dizzy and stunned, she could do nothing but gasp for air as the man danced about, frantically batting at something that writhed between his legs.

*A snake*, she realized as she massaged her bruised throat. *It's a snake.*

With a sickening crunch, the handler stomped the serpent's head – and kept stomping long after it ceased moving. Panting hard, he looked at Alenka not with triumph, but horror.

His eyes rolled, and he slumped to the ground.

Though Alenka should have expected it, she gasped as the snake corpse began to bubble with ink-black smoke. It gathered into a vortex, then hurled itself at the handler's face. It did so twice more, before coming to hover impatiently in front of Alenka.

From the hall, urgent footsteps approached.

Alenka crept forward and placed a hand on the man's neck. His pulse was rapid and erratic, his breath a labored wheeze. She knew what the shadow-thing wanted.

"It's mercy," she told herself as she pinched the man's nose and covered his mouth. "He's in pain. He's already dying." But when he spasmed his last, and the light left his eyes, no words could change the fact she'd killed him.

The moment she lifted her hands, the shadow-thing rushed in, inhaled by the dead man. Alenka slinked back from it. The corpse stretched, testing its limbs, and rose to its feet. Lazily, it picked up the dagger.

"What is the meaning of this?" came a shout from behind them.

Standing in the doorway was the Divinus. Two guards flanked him, jaws slack at the scene of destruction.

"Truly, girl," the priest hissed, "you make this too easy." He shook his head at Alenka, and turned to the handler. "Jodah, return the Deadspeaker to her chamber. She has profaned the sanctum with her lies, and for this, the dead have driven her mad."

The corpse's hand clamped Alenka's shoulder, and, with a shove, guided her forward. She glanced back in dismay…

…and saw its gaze flick discreetly to the torches.

As they inched forward, she could sense the dead thing straining to advance.

"Come now," snapped the Divinus. "I gave you an order."

Alenka lurched free of the corpse's grasp. She seized the nearest torch and snuffed it against the ground. She grabbed another and did the same.

Too late, the Divinus realized what she was doing. "Stop her!" he cried.

But it had been enough. Freed of the ring of light, the dead thing sprung forth, dagger flashing. The guards beat at it with fists and clubs, but if it felt any pain, it didn't show it. With a sudden spray of red, both were down.

"Jodah?" stammered the Divinus, inching back from the stalking corpse. "What has she offered you? I'll better it! I'll–"

His words cut off in a strangled cry as the dead thing caught his throat and squeezed. He beat at its arms, at its face, but was powerless against its unrelenting strength. His eyes bulged. His face purpled.

And then he shuddered, and was no more.

Only then did Alenka remember to inhale. She found herself surrounded by death, pinned by the accusing stares of the fallen guards. She skittered back on hands and feet, scuttling like a crab.

What monster had she released from its prison?

To her surprise, it was not the priest, but the handler, Jodah, who slumped to the floor. The Divinus cocked his head left and right, as if working out a stiff neck. He reached a hand toward Alenka...

And screamed.

*Shall we?* said the dead thing.

Despite the late hour, no one questioned the Divinus as he left the temple. And no one troubled the acolyte who followed, head bowed, at his heels.

As they walked the moonlit road in silence, Alenka suppressed an urge to run. Even when the temple was lost to sight, obscured by the shadows of trees, she couldn't stop trembling. Though she'd feared the Divinus, the horror that stalked beside her, wearing his skin, was a thousand times worse.

And she had set it loose upon the world.

For just a moment, she rested her weary eyes – and snapped them back open. Each time she let them droop, the accusing stares of the dead were waiting.

She had killed them, one with her own hands.

Something large moved in the nearby brush, nearly stopping Alenka's heart.

The dead thing gazed into the forest, as if shadow were no impediment to its vision. A knowing grin crept over its face. It turned to Alenka, nodded once, and departed.

Though, thankfully, the dead thing hadn't spoken, Alenka understood she was not meant to follow. She couldn't peel her eyes from its retreating form until long after it was swallowed by the darkness. When at last she turned back to the source of the noise, she caught a glint of moonlight on something metal. Her heart leapt.

It was a silver circlet.

Kiara emerged from the brush, leading her horse by the bridle. "Is he gone?"

The nervous excitement, the relief, the fear she'd barely held in check, all washed over Alenka in a flood of tears. She threw her arms around a girl she barely knew, and wept. "You came! Thank the gods. I wasn't sure you would."

The Lady Theron – that's who Kiara was, now, Alenka realized – hugged her close. "I'm a fool for a damsel in distress, and can only guess what you risked for me. I saw the priest's rage when you spoke your verdict. I half expected him to declare it false and denounce you on the spot."

Alenka stepped back and wiped her nose with a sniffle. "He nearly did. But it's okay now."

Kiara stared down the road, curiosity etched plainly on her face, but the Divinus was nowhere to be seen. She shrugged. "Come, we'd better get out of here."

Together they climbed into the saddle. Alenka clung to Kiara's waist, leaning close to breathe her scent of horses and meadow grass. It was the scent of freedom.

As they set off into the night, Kiara gave one last glance behind her. "I still can't believe the Divinus let you go. Do you think, with you out of the way, he'll change your verdict?"

"Trust me," Alenka said. "He won't do that."

*He can't,* she thought, *because the dead don't lie.*

*Chris Cornetto is a physics teacher by day and writer by night. In addition to physics, he has degrees in chemistry, philosophy, and psychology. He likes exploring ethical questions through fantasy settings, and enjoys long walks with small dogs. His work has appeared in several magazines, including Metaphorosis, Hypnos, and DreamForge, and his novella, "The Door in the Mountain," is forthcoming through Of Metal and Magic press. He was also a finalist for the 2022 Baen Fantasy Adventure Award.*

# Parasitoid

*Nicholas G. Marconi*

At first I was confused. Why would someone so far out of my league invite me over?

But she smelled so good I left my better judgement at the bar.

She sat me down on the bed. Her smile, intoxicating. Her kiss, captivating. Her smell— oh God, her smell! I wanted to stay there forever.

That's why I didn't move when she left, or when she came back and buried the egg in my chest. It's why I'm still here three days later as the damn thing is hatching.

Everything about this is excruciating. And yet...

It smells like her...

*Nicholas G. Marconi's story "A Recipe For You In The New World" was the winner of NYC Midnight's 2022 100-Word Microfiction Challenge, and it is part of Apex Magazine's Strange Libations anthology. HIs drabble "Two-Star Yelp Review of Mermaid Lagoon" appears in Fairfield Scribes Issue # 27.*

# The Quiet and the Creeping
*Jalyn Renae Fiske*

Our daughter wants me to move to a place where I can be watched over. I try to tell her that I'm already being watched over, by the Quiet People, but she doesn't believe me when I say they exist.

She pretends not to hear and says, "Mamá, it will be nice and clean there." Is cleanliness all that matters? I know Lupe is talking about sending me to an old folks' home. The air will be too cold and the chairs hard and un-lived in. And it would smell of antiseptic layered over urine like every nursing home and hospital. That's not what I want, but Lupe won't listen. How could I abandon all that I know and love? I would miss the Quiet People and my bed with the coral quilt. Pictures of you, me, and our Lupe on the walls.

She used to be so little. I remember when she asked us every question that popped in her head. Mamá, why can't I go to the stars today? What does a praying mantis pray about? Can we dig for dinosaur bones in the backyard? Now the only things she asks me are if I slept well and did I take my medicine. When I try to talk to her of my *real* thoughts, of *real* things, she says, "Oh, Mamá," and checks the fridge for expired food and the air filter for too much dust before running off to tend to her own life. I don't blame her. I wish to tend to my own life, too.

Outside my window, I sometimes see lonely men and weeping women visiting the Quiet People in St. Peregrine Cemetery across the road. I pretend they are also here to visit me. Like the man in faded jeans and grey coat who comes at least twice a week. Always smoking, that one. I named him Francisco because he reminds me so much of you.

People used to say, "Clarinda, what a lucky woman you are! Francisco is such a gentleman!" It's true. I never worried about you drinking at the bar and driving home drunk like so many other wives worried about. You were always quicker to cry at something beautiful than to rage in anger at something upsetting. But I haven't heard your name uttered from someone's lips in a very long time. Not even my own name.

Well, that's not completely true. Sometimes the phone rings, and I wonder if it might be Lupe, so I answer, "Mija, is that you?" But a stranger's voice responds: "Granny Clarinda, it's me." I chuckle because I'm not an abuela. I keep asking Lupe when she'll give us a grandchild, but it hasn't happened yet. "Don't you remember?" the voice says, "I'm your grandson…David." Or they might say Ben or John or James. They always want money, but I don't fall for it. Someday I might. Someday when I've been alone for too long and I don't remember where I am or who I am, I'll be so happy to learn I have a mijito who calls me that I'll give them what they want. I'll give them every penny as payment for their love.

I wake up at odd hours, *wrong* hours, when I should still be sleeping. This is how I know I'm being watched over. All is quiet, yet I know someone else is awake, just outside my window. The thought that I'm not alone is comforting, but I feel anxious like I'm committing a crime if I look outside. Wrapped in my coral quilt, I find the courage to peer into St. Peregrine and see the Quiet People weaving their wispy bodies among the gravestones. A dance at midnight. I call them the Quiet People because they never speak, never scream or yell at each other, or blare their television sets into the early morning.

Tonight, the Quiet People are walking the labyrinth at the center of the cemetery. A replica, it is said, of a famous French labyrinth in Chartres Cathedral. The stone path is coiled back and forth like a rope or a snake so that when you approach the center and you think you're close, the stones pull you away, back to the very edge. You see, Francisco, it is not until you are the furthest away that you suddenly find yourself finished and standing in the labyrinth's heart. Isn't that lovely and strange? A sign posted next to the maze says to walk in prayer, and once you find the heart, your prayer will be answered. I think I might like to walk the labyrinth. If I were to do it, I would ask: When can I die?

Lupe apologized for celebrating my birthday a day late. Her work schedule has been crazy. I understand. She makes time to take me to all my doctor's appointments even though she works two jobs. She works so hard, our Lupe, just like you did for us.

She brought me a homemade pound cake, or is it rum? I think I'm losing the ability to taste things. I wish I had more people to share my cake with, but I've outlived too many. The world is full of strangers. Lupe asks about my health and stock of food, but that isn't what I want to talk about. "I'd rather be dead than in a nursing home," I say. "I've lived a long life. It doesn't bother me." Lupe sighs and averts her eyes, fluffs some pillows on the couch. "It's not good that you live so close to a cemetery," she says. "It would depress me, too."

I'm not depressed. When I was fourteen, I looked forward to my quinceanera. And at fifteen, to when I could drive. I welcomed falling in love, getting married, having a child. Milestones. Chapters. Am I supposed to ignore the final chapter? The ending is what makes everything that came before make sense. And I want mine to be a good one.

Midnight. The Quiet People weave among the gravestones, and from my window, I watch them under the star-studded night. They begin to form a line, one after the other, and approach the labyrinth. It reminds me of the time long ago when you took me to see a ballet on stage, *Swan Lake*, and the dancers glided about, weightless, with scarves of silk fluttering behind them. Just like that, six of my cemetery friends walk the stone maze several paces behind each other. Sometimes it's three or four, but never just one. When the leader reaches the heart, they bow their head and disappear, but not in an abrupt way. There's a fading, a rippling outward. I shouldn't be looking. I shouldn't even be awake. One of the Quiet People reaches the center, the corazon, and looks up at my window instead of down, her bright eyes meeting my own hazy ones, and then disappears. They all disappear.

I feel as though I've been stuck in this little house and this little room my whole life. I go for a walk, even though I can't walk too far without having to stop and rest my legs and back, catch my breath. That's probably why only Lupe visits me. I'm too slow for this fast world, but slow is as fast as I can go. The gate is unlocked today and open just enough. I want some company, not conversation. The Quiet People are there at St. Peregrine, even though they're hard to see in sunlight. I can feel them, and they aren't too fast for someone like me. They're very good at waiting.

A few years ago, when I wasn't such a nuisance, I would drive to the grocery store when I didn't need food, and I'd talk to the workers there. Sometimes the customers, too. Dozens of people, so lively and young. "Oh, hello, Clarinda," the manager would say with a smile. Her name was Chelsea, the same age as our Lupe. Chelsea was promoted to a newer, bigger store in a newer, bigger town. I continued to go to the store almost daily, but with Chelsea gone, they hardly looked at me, only nodded in passing like I was a child. And suddenly I was even more alone than before, surrounded by so many people.

But not here in St. Peregrine. I wander among the ivy and graffiti-covered gravestones. Toppled tombstones, sliced in half. Names and messages painted over and lost to time, but I can still make out a few of them. *A beautiful star shines over the grave, of one we loved but could not save.* I wonder what they will say of me when I'm gone.

I wake up in my bed, shivering as if it were snowing right inside my room. The cold finds me no matter if I layer on more sweaters and socks, add more blankets, or turn up the heater. It clings to my every breath. When I manage to swing my feet to the floor, I see the cemetery mud caked between my toes and buried inside each delicate wrinkle of skin. My feet are the only part of me not frozen, and I remember it wasn't cold out by the labyrinth. When I watched the dance of the Quiet People, I was as warm as if I were young again, curled up by a crackling fire and snuggled in a quilt. My window is covered in lacy ribbons of ice, and I know where I must go.

I am out in the cemetery all night, touching every gravestone, reading each name. The Quiet People stay hidden, but I know they watch over me like guardian angels. The cold chill of midnight never reaches my bones. I think about walking the labyrinth, but I feel a tug backward. Not today. Not yet.

When the sun emerges, and I no longer feel the warmth of their eyes and attention, I decide to return home. Standing in the living room is Lupe overwhelmed with worry. She's always frowning now. Stressed. On edge. "Where have you been?" she cries. "I was about to call the police!" I went for a walk, I tell her, but I know that nothing I say will be what she wants to hear. Lupe's voice grows louder. "In your nightgown?"

I'm a child again, and she the parent.

Lupe assigns me a curfew of six o'clock in the evening, and I'm not allowed to leave the house without her permission. She takes my car keys, even though my Cadillac, parked in the driveway, has gathered at least a year's worth of dust and leaves. I wonder if she'll take the house keys, too. Lock me in. Carve my epitaph on the door: *Here rests Clarinda, though she tried so hard to get away.* I don't know what to say, so Lupe leaves to go to work. I think I hear "I love you," but I'm not sure. She doesn't turn around.

I catch their shadows among the trees. Their sparkling eyes in the sky. The Quiet People are bolder, stronger, more visible even in the sun. It must be because no one visits St. Peregrine's like they used to, not even the one I named after you. I haven't seen him in ages. The wrought iron gates surrounding the cemetery remain closed, like an abandoned theme park that people lost interest in. The fewer of the living who come, the more the Quiet People venture out, walk the labyrinth, and disappear. But I'm still here. I'm still here.

The cuckoo clock you gave me on our first anniversary chirps at noon. The sound makes me think of lunch, so I walk to the kitchen even though I'm not actually hungry. My days have melted into one single hour, neither day nor night, neither mealtime nor nap time. Still, I should eat. The bread box contains white, moldy bread, but I ate a sandwich just yesterday. Or was that a week ago? It doesn't matter. I eat a slice of moldy bread anyway. It tastes of sand. I turn to tell Lupe this, that food only tastes of sand, but no one is in the kitchen. I suppose silence is there. It follows me like a little servant, quickly snatching up every sound I make as if I'm not really moving or breathing or being. I walk into my room and turn to tell Lupe I feel hollow, my very soul hollowed out, but it's only me. And the silence. I look out the window and into the darkness. Wasn't it just noon? Now it is midnight. I sit in the chair and pull my coral quilt tight around me. I'm not cold, no, but it's what I always do before I cry.

It's not that I am forgetting things. I've just stopped caring. Lupe has taken me to an old folks' home, where it smells of anti-septic and urine and baby powder. I'm miles away from St. Peregrine's and the Quiet People. Now when I look out my window, I see concrete where there should be grass.

A woman named Dolores lives the next room over, and Ruth is just across the hall. Dolores is nearly deaf and plays her records as loud as she can. My favorite is when she plays "Stand By Me" by Ben E. King after dinner. Tonight it was meatloaf, creamed corn, and mushy peas. I can't bring myself to eat. With so few days left to live, why would I waste the effort on something so disappointing? I want deliciousness in my final moments. I want laughter and smiles and chocolate and cake. You used to make the most lovely tres leches.

Did I tell you? Lupe learned how to cook your famous enchiladas by heart, no recipe. She made them last Christmas. That was a nice day. The kitchen smelled like you, sounded like you. I miss our home. I forgot to bring my coral quilt, can you believe that? You wouldn't want me here, without our daughter, without my friends.

Sometimes, though, I think that maybe they followed me here, the Quiet People. When I used to see them walking the labyrinth, their eyes seemed to glow, and I've seen the same kind of thing here. At night, when the orderlies and nurses are mostly gone, I've seen a dark face look in through the small window on my door. Its eyes reflect the light like a cat's, but they're not yellow. The eyes are white. I wave, but it continues to stare, unblinking. Only when I look away and pretend to go to sleep does it eventually turn and disappear from view. I call Lupe to tell her what I saw, but no one answers. It's late. I'll try again tomorrow.

Every night, the same dark face stares at me from the hallway. I can't describe the features. There is nothing distinguishable, save for the white, reflecting eyes. I stop waving when it comes. When I wave is when it stares. The Quiet People never did that. Their eyes glowed a warm amber, like the cooling coals of a fire.

I ask Dolores if she's seen them, but she shakes her head and looks away. Pretends not to hear me. I know she can hear me. I saw her talking with Ruth during the day, and no one had to yell to be heard. I ask Dolores again—"Are you sure you haven't seen anything?" but she only responds, "The music is nice, isn't it? How it blocks everything out?" Ruth shuffles over to us as the nurses announce bedtime. "Dolores won't tell you anything. She thinks they watch us even in the daylight. She thinks they're listening to us right now." Are they? She tells me to ask again in the morning. She'll tell me all about the Creeping Ones then.

Breakfast the next morning is mushy eggs—they call it scrambled—mushy hashbrowns and soggy toast. Dolores sits with me. We watch our orange juice glasses sweat and condensate as our food grows cold. The seat for Ruth remains ominously empty. I begin to ask Dolores if she thinks something happened, but she shakes her head rapidly, her gray curls bouncing this way and that. "Ruth hates waking up."

It isn't until half past eleven that Ruth emerges and joins us on one of the couches in the common room. "It's still morning," she says, eyeing the clock on the wall. "As long as you're up by noon, they don't mind. The nurses and such, they'll leave you be. That's when you should sleep, by the way, is from six to just before noon. Dolores has her own routine with the music, but I'd rather keep watch. If they're watching me, you can bet I'm watching them." Them? "The Creeping Ones, of course." All night? "All night." Can they hurt you? "If you leave your door open, sure. That's what they're doing, you know. Creeping up and down the halls, checking for open doors." What do they want? "Well, in." But why? "Honey, I haven't asked them."

I'm not surprised by any of this because I know of the Quiet People, but while they invoke feelings of magic and warmth, the Creeping Ones are dread and cold. I feel like telling Lupe what I learned, but my call goes to voicemail. I've missed her calls, too. She left a message promising to come see me, but it's an empty kind of promise, an apology for all the other visits she's missed over the years. More of a wish than anything. I'm starting to forget her face. I know her voice so well; just her voice.

Lupe wants to visit me, I'm sure of it, but there are ten other things she wants more. Isn't that how the world works? This is nothing out of the ordinary. I leave her a message: "Lupe, I hope things are okay with you. I miss you. If you visit me, please come during the day. It's not good at night here. The Creeping Ones, they— oh, well, nevermind that. Just come during the day. When it's bright. Good and bright."

Ruth doesn't join us on the couch today. Dolores and I are watching *The Waltons* on the television when I say, "Did you hear the rattling last night? So many door knobs being turned. I could barely sleep." Dolores shakes her head. Of course not. She has her music. I'd wanted to go check the hallway and see what was going on, but a Creeping One was at my door, peering in for hours. Maybe that's what they do. They each guard a room, locking us in. But I could have sworn I heard a door creak open and closed. At lunch, I notice the nurses bringing a gurney to Ruth's room. Stroke, they say.

Lupe keeps saying she'll come visit as soon as she gets some time off. It's quite a drive to get to me from where she lives. If we were closer, things would be different. I don't want to be a bother. Dolores stays in her room more than ever now, blaring her music. I've asked for paper and paint and pens—whatever they have here—and I spend my time drawing the labyrinth and the Quiet People, the scene I used to watch out my window every night and often during the day. I think if I can fill the room with it, it will be like being back

there, and maybe there won't be any Creeping Ones anymore. Just the Quiet. Or, at least it will occupy my mind. It feels good to *do* something. I'm not so lonely as long as I have something to do, someone to talk with. That's what Lupe doesn't understand. I just want to talk with her, to sit with her, to know she's near. I wouldn't be a bother.

I've drawn at least fifty mazes now. One wall is full. My hands are shaky, but the image is clear. I can see my friends again. Another death happens in the night, a man named Leonard. He outlived his wife and children, so there is no one to notify. Do you see that, Francisco—the Creeping One at my door—doesn't it look like Ruth? Wide-set eyes, droopy mouth. I swear it's her, and I'm tempted to let her in. It seems like she wants to talk with me, and I have so much to tell her. I haven't talked to anyone in ages.

Dolores's record player stopped working. Instead of music, there is silence. I worry for her, but she says she'll sing to herself instead to keep the Creeping Ones at bay. But for how long? She can't sing for eternity. While I've been here, we've lost Ruth, then Leonard, and now this morning, Janek. I've seen them all, walking the halls, staring with their shadowy faces and white, white eyes.

I've drawn so many Quiet People and their labyrinths by now my whole room is covered, even the floor. But it isn't enough, is it? I'm cocooning. I'm safe, but is Dolores? Or Maria Louisa or Irene? I know I'll be seeing them next, one by one, becoming a Creeping One, and watching me with their aching eyes, pleading that I open the door. Why is that, Francisco? Maybe they're looking for somewhere to go. All that pacing in the hallways, looking into windows, gripping the knobs. The Quiet People walk at night, too. But they have a path to follow, a place to go.

I know they think I'm crazy. This is an old folks' home, but it might as well be an asylum, too. Half of the residents can't remember their family or their neighbors or themselves. I don't see how that means it's fine to let them die so alone, and then to wander in such a state. I told all this to Dolores. Her throat is raw from singing all night and her eyes rimmed red from staying awake. She agrees to help me draw the labyrinth. I have it memorized, and I've drawn it so many times now that it'll be easy. We'll use chalk from the craft cart in the common room and make a path that leads right to the maze. Clear the furniture and draw it right there on the floor. The nurses, though, they see my room and all the drawings I've done and think I'm insane. We'll have to do it right after bedtime, when the Creeping Ones first start to come out. I can do it. I'll do it for Ruth and everyone who is looking for a way out, and I'll do it for Dolores, who isn't ready to go yet. And then I can tell Lupe all about how I turned the Creeping Ones into the Quiet People and that they were real all along.

The hardest part about drawing the labyrinth isn't having to crawl on my hands and knees. It hurts, yes, but the hardest part is locking the Creeping Ones in the empty rooms, so I have time to draw. Dolores and I open all the doors we can where no one was living, even hers and mine, and when a Creeping One walks in, we shut the door quick. I'm not sure how long it will hold them, but I figure if they can't get *in*, then they can't get *out*.

The night nurses see Dolores and me in the hallway and say, "It's time to sleep, ladies," to which I say, "I left my book in the common room. I'll just get it now." Dolores nods to me and whispers that she'll stay back and open the doors when I'm done. I tell her I'll sing a tune when it's time—"Stand by Me." That makes her smile.

I don't know how long it takes to draw the labyrinth. I keep at it even though my knees ache, my wrists pinch painfully, even my chest grows tight and my breath short. It's so hard to breathe, but I finish. It's done. The labyrinth is chalked on the floor from wall to wall, ready to be walked.

I stand up and sing. Softly, just so Dolores can hear me. But nothing happens. I keep singing. Dolores must have fallen asleep. I walk into the dark hallway. The nurses are gone, probably doing inventory. A single door is open, its light spilling out. I see Dolores's feet with their purple socks. She must have fallen. "Dolores?" I call. She doesn't rise. A Creeping One hears me and comes out of the room, wearing Dolores's round face and her curly white hair. It takes me a moment to react.

How can my friends die so quickly? And with so much silence? No goodbyes. "Follow me," I say, and she does. I let out the others—Ruth and Leonard and Janek and even a few more I didn't know—and lead them to the common room. I'd hoped they would know what to do when they saw the labyrinth, but they walk to the windows instead. Looking at their ghostly reflections, I suppose. They do have reflections. Their faces meld with the night, but their white eyes flash back, unseeing yet seeing all.

I will have to show them how it's done. "This way," I say and begin to walk the labyrinth. Ruth tears herself from the window first and follows, then Dolores and the rest. If I stop walking, so do they. We are a chain of souls, linked, connected by invisible threads. I will have to go to the very center. And then what? I'd dreamed of following the Quiet People in St. Peregrine's and walking the labyrinth with them, but I never thought I'd actually make it to the end. Or that I would be the one leading.

As I walk, I pass by what looks like me asleep on the floor, but that can't be. I am here, in the maze, my feet so sure of where to go. My final thoughts are of our Lupe, and how I wish things had been different for us after you died. When I reach the corazon, everything goes warm and amber, like crackling coals.

I wake up back home, in our bed, beneath my coral quilt. Lupe brings me some sliced strawberries with chocolate syrup drizzled on top and fusses over the pillows. Is that propped up enough for you? Are you warm? I realize now how much I miss that about her. And then she sits down next to me on the bed and takes my hands in hers.

I remember this moment. I've lived it before. It was the day after your funeral.

We sit there like that for a while, no rushing, no sighing. "Lupe," I say. "I know you have to go back to work now. You work so hard." That's when her sigh comes, but it sounds different than how I remember it being. It sounds sad. Has it always been sad?

Our Lupe says, "Oh, Mamá. It's a lot to pay for two homes and take care of everything by myself, that's all. I wish I could visit you more." And something I'd always wanted but never said—only, I say it now—comes out of my mouth. "Why must you visit? If we lived together, we'd see each other every day."

I expect her to stand up and check the lightbulbs and the pantry and the trash bins, but this time she doesn't. She stays right there with me and says quietly, "I thought you said you'd never leave your house and your things. My place is so small." Her chin drops, her eyes fall. "And it's just me there."

Did she do that often? Look down? I don't think I'd ever really seen her when she came by. I was always looking out the window.

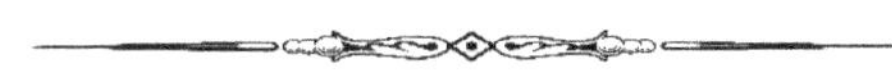

*Jalyn Renae Fiske is a speculative fiction author of Mexican heritage residing in Texas. She earned her MFA in Creative Writing in 2017 and is an alum of the Gunn Center for the Study of Science Fiction as well as the Ad Astra Center for the Speculative Imagination at the University of Kansas. Jalyn serves as Fiction Editor for the magazine James Gunn's Ad Astra, and her work has appeared in Mythaxis, The Overcast, Typehouse, The Future Fire, and in anthologies from Rogue Blades Entertainment and Transmundane Press. Her writing leans toward fantasy and psychological horror and explores themes of loss, otherness, and challenging status quos. Often, her writing calls out harmful societal constructs and asks the reader to re-examine what they value and what they disregard--and why.*

# Repairs
### *David McGillveray*

Benek found it brought him some peace, coming out to the edge. No obstacles, no anomalies, no other racers, just him and the wind and the drop. He rolled forward, feeling the smooth surface beneath his tyres and the hum of the engine, closer and closer until the precipice was only centimetres away.

The side of the platform rose sheer for a kilometre above Epaulette's empty ocean. He lowered a window and looked over, feeling the urge to just fall away, to be swallowed in gulfs of air, to let clouds enshroud his body. He stopped the car and eased back in his seat, bathing in the evening light of Ukanka, its raspberry and vanilla bands hanging so huge in the sky that it felt as if he could reach out and take a scoop of ice cream from the gas giant's atmosphere.

The radio chimed on the hour, tuned to the race channel for alerts.

*"Attention individuals! The registration window for the next contest is now closed and no more tenders may be made. Racers, prepare to display your speed and panache. There are now forty-eight hours til race time, forty-eight hours til race time! Spectacle, wealth and adoration await!"*

Benek inhaled a long, shuddering breath, suddenly overcome. A wave of pain pulsed through his body as if on cue, a reminder. Well, he would need that pain to keep him sharp. His name was on that race register now and he couldn't take it back.

He breathed out and wiped wetness from his eyes. At an instruction through the neural link that connected them, the racer injected a soporific directly into his spine. He closed his eyes and slept a not-quite-sleep, rocked by the wind.

The world spinning as he lost control. The looming mass of an alien figure and the terrible crunch of impact. Depthless hurting. Flames and the sickening stink of burning meat. His own voice, screaming.

Rondolo's Corner was a neon carbuncle growing on the platform's most south-westerly point. Benek drove his racer slowly down the main drag eating an ice cream. The town was home to gawpers, loners, chancers and thrill-seekers, to people from all across the system who wanted a taste of the alien or who had just run out of road. Benek considered he was not so different. The xeno-archaeologists, long discouraged by the platform's disinclination to give up its secrets, rarely visited any more.

Rondolo himself, an anarchist and promoter of the outlaw spirit, had tried to foist his philosophies on the culture that grew up around the races before he had disappeared. But in the few years since, that idealism had quickly devolved and mutated into something more craven; a cavalier callousness, a casual disregard for everything but the credit in your account.

Light and music spilled from bars and cheap hotels. Garish advertisements shimmered in the air, touting the motor-chop-shops supporting the races or the many ways along the strip of getting off your face. Augmented sluts! Tailored hallucinations! Every hour is happy hour!

Bins overflowed and trash filled the gutters; smashed glass and exhausted stim patches, fast food wrappers and brown cigarillo butts. The air wafting through Benek's window was intense with drug smoke, perfumed pheromones and shouting. It was always like this the night before race day, the whole tilt of the place changed and rolling around crazy.

Stoners and whores watched him from upstairs balconies. A few shouted his name. He was known here and he tried to bite down on the little thrill that still gave him. Despite it all, it was good to be back. Couldn't deny it.

Half way up the drag festered the Glittering Pig, the eponymous beast performing a glitching hologrammatic dance in the sky, raising its pork-pie hat on endless repeat. A canopy facing on to the street covered a collection of plastic chairs and chipped formica tables three-quarters filled with punters. As Benek drew level, the whistles and the calling started. They were all there, as he knew they would be, surrounded by smoke and hangers-on. He pulled to a stop, made his engine purr.

"Hey, Benek, you coming in for a drink? Come sit in my lap, baby." That was Adaeze, clad in black plastic, her short green dreads glittering with silver lights, enough rings in her ears to cover all her fingers and toes. Some laughter at that. They had been together, once.

They were all there, though, Vayne, Harmer and the rest. Bullies at the school gate.

Then Mercere himself stood and leaned grinning across their table. Driving visor permanently grafted over his eyes, depilated skull inlaid with gold, muscled chest under an open leather waistcoat. "Hey, Wipeout's back in town," he shouted. Everyone was looking now. More laughter. "Have to say, never thought I'd see your name on the race list again. Last time I looked you were burning in my rear-view cameras."

Benek made sure he held their stares, the faces turned harder now. He had chosen to come here, to face them.

"No? Nothing?" Mercere called. "Lost your voice along with everything else? Don't matter, listen to me. Most important thing you lost that day was your rep and you can't buy that back. The great Nuffi Benek is *gone*, man. I'll see you go out for sure this time."

There came a chorus of hollers and catcalls from the crowd, the clinking of glasses.

Benek nodded and finished his ice cream, rolled on down the strip.

Race day. Twelve competitors lined up in the shadow of the raptor under a ceiling of pink clouds. The raptor, a human-made sculpture twenty metres tall made from mangled car parts, was a poor imitation of the alien figures that formed the maze. Monitor drones hung overhead like severed plastic heads studded with sensor eyes and network icons. Platform races were syndicated all across the system, cashflows accruing to a cabal of media barons. But enough trickled down to change the lives of race winners.

*"Attention individuals! Racers, T minus five for the ninety-ninth platform derby, T minus five. The course, determined today by System Six Media, will now be uploaded to your in-vehicle displays. No collusion, no deals, no projectiles, just speed and élan!"*

Benek grunted as he studied the route. It was never released until immediately before the start, but over thirty races, twenty of them placed finishes, Benek's knowledge of what lay out there was the equal of anyone's. Since the crash he had spent days out there alone, obsessively covering the ground, building maps in his mind, making it his home. He marked the course's different options, its forks and twists, where it passed through zones where strange things happened.

"Ready to feel the heat again, Wipeout?"

Benek looked over the noses of the other racers to where his rival's electric blue supertrike sat exhaling coolant. Mercere was hunched forward over the vehicle's controls, not caring to look over, skull gleaming.

Benek felt the knotting in his guts as the clock counted down, distracting himself with last minute diagnostics he knew he didn't need. His hands shook on the wheel until he clenched them hard and forced himself to control his breathing. Then there was nothing left but the final seconds passing in an agony of retarded time.

*"GO!"*

The contenders streaked across the flat, each trying to get an early advantage. Benek focused along the tapering green nose of his racer, feeling it cut the air, feeling the power in his engine. He could see the edge of the maze a kilometre ahead, a borderland of twisted *things* spun from impossible materials, of melted colossi and enigmatic machines caught in their final moments, millennia past.

He was well ahead of the pack, had left them behind in a chicane formed by snaking alien polyps the size of freight trains. Eyes flicking to the route indicated on his screens, he chose a fork he had taken in previous races and hit the accelerator again.

A tyre hit what must have been an imploder charge and the front of his racer just *crumpled*, his velocity carrying the rest of it through in an uncontrollable skid, then a tumble as it flipped. Pain lanced through his legs and up his spine like nothing he could ever have imagined. Through streaked tears he glimpsed Mercere and Adaeze flash past before he was crushed against the foot of the Totem, it's precarious tower of melted alien skulls indifferent to the flames licking at his body.

A tortured eternity separated the moment of the crash from the moment his door was wrenched off and the rescue team were spraying fire retardant over him and yelling in his face.

"Stay with me, racer boy, look at me. Shit, hold this. It's bad, man, really bad. We'll have to cut him free."

Benek's single word could have been his dying breath: "No."

He relived those memories again and again. All the drugs, the medical machines, the months of therapy, none of it had taken them away. But against all the forecasts, Benek was back amongst it. Racing. He felt like he had a chance again and that felt good, the ground flashing by beneath his chassis, rivals in his screens.

As soon as he entered the maze the hum of his engine seemed to deepen and he felt the familiar strangeness, the peculiar atmosphere, an unsettling sense of *observation*. He felt like it knew him as well as he knew it, like an unreliable friend.

The platform's surface was a perfect obsidian square fifty kilometres on a side sitting alone in the middle of Epaulette's ocean, the only artefact found in the entire system despite the presence of three other habitable biospheres. The course curled for over eighty kilometres through its bizarre interior, among its nested mysteries.

There were as many theories as there were drunks. Crowds of inhuman refugees waiting to be lifted off-world by rescuers who never came. A mustering army fried by some apocalyptic weapon. An alien sculpture park. A memorial? The drivers' favourite was that it was a game board for the children of some lost super-race. One of those children had been a sore loser and ruined the pieces for everyone else in a fit of pique, abandoning the game forever.

Benek could understand that type of mentality. He need only look at Mercere.

He sped beneath the figure nicknamed Pennine's Spitter. The thing stood five storeys tall, three massive trunk-like legs supporting a crazed web-work of twisted strands suddenly sheared off at the top. Five blood red beads the size of human children hung suspended in the air above it devoid of any apparent energy source.

Mercere was ahead of him, pulling away in a fearsome burst of acceleration.

He was not the only one. Benek, more cautious, feeling his way back into the groove, kept to the middle of the way. Walls of alien material like some impenetrable fairy-tale forest narrowed ahead, forcing the racers through a bottleneck.

Benek's instincts kicked in as he felt Adaeze bearing down on him from the rear before he even saw her in his cameras. With a command through the neural link, his racer leapt ahead and Adaeze's bumper merely touched his own, a kiss rather than the hammer blow she had intended. Her rig was massive, a pimped landcruiser the size of a powerboat, windscreen opaque, a bloody maw decorating its front grille.

He left her behind. He was confident there wasn't a vehicle out there who could match him on the straight, not after all the enhancements he had introduced. He was remade!

The course doglegged left and opened out onto a plaza kilometres across marked on the maps as the Giving Ground. Drones swooped. Benek tore past three rivals who had taken advantage of his hesitant start, one of them Harmer, the sleek black shard of his racer humming close to the ground. Harmer tried to sideswipe him but Benek deftly braked then accelerated again, shunting him up the backside. He spun out. Benek raced on.

Mercere disappeared back into the maze on the far side, Benek pursuing him like a starved predator. He could feel the old fire rising in him now, the adrenalin coursing stronger than any other drug, the action knitting him together.

Into bright white light where none should be. The sky disappeared. Giant hands seemed to grab at him from white mist before shattering, ephemeral. A deep base vibration throbbed in the very air around him, like the sounding of some colossal sea-beast. He couldn't think, suddenly couldn't see. Instinctively he applied full pressure to the brakes, his torso thrown forward against the wheel with a surge of pain. He closed his eyes…

…and opened them. His engine hummed quietly. Ukanka's raspberry light seeped through clouds overhead. An octopoid monstrosity stood to his right, one arm raised in greeting/warning. He blinked. The thing was above him, damaged and dead like all the other pieces on the game board. He shook his head to clear it. He knew this place. It was a kilometre from the course and he was facing the wrong way.

Racers claimed to have exited the maze before they had entered it. They'd been tailed by odd lights and living shadows, had been teleported across tens of kilometres, found themselves inexplicably retracing their own path. Some, like Rondolo, has simply never come back out. Benek himself had experienced odd lensing effects before, gaps in his memory. This had been the worst.

He U-turned and headed at speed back into the maze, progressing unhindered until his displays told him he had rejoined the course. He passed racer after racer, his machine and reflexes superior, controlling everything at the speed of instinct. Benek pushed two hundred kilometres an hour, surging across the game board's open spaces and firing along narrow avenues lined with cyborg carcasses and frozen horrors, the light changing constantly as if the cycle of Epaulette's days and nights had come unstuck. The whole platform seemed alive with strange energy.

He saw race drones hovering ahead like vultures. Smoke rose from the mangled metal corpse of a racer jammed under the feet of another of the platform's giant sculptures. Benek couldn't make out who it was as he flew past.

And then he saw Adaeze again, ahead of him now, dominating the road. He could tell at once from the micro-movements of her vehicle she knew he was there. He chased her into a tunnel formed as the reaching, outstretched arms of titanic chrome fungi met and merged overhead. Benek turned on his lights and immediately felt his wheels slide beneath him as, too late, he spotted the slick she'd released. He rushed towards Adaeze's larger vehicle as she slammed on her brakes, fought to avoid a collision and was forced along the side of the tunnel, the awful screech of tearing metal filling the confined space as he ripped along the wall in a fountain of sparks.

Benek gasped as all the old terror rose up again. His racer finally broke free and came to a halt slewed across the way, lights chasing shadows along the tunnel walls.

Adaeze's engine roared and her voice came from his radio. "Surprise, Benek. No glorious return for—"

But there was something wrong with it. Her voice was slurred, slowed down. Still groggy, he squinted at her cruiser, waiting thirty metres back down the track. It was swathed in a glowing cloud of fireflies. He thought they were the sparks thrown up from his collision with the wall, somehow gathered up. A wind whistled down the tunnel and the sparks swirled slowly about Adaeze's vehicle, flecks of gold stirred through white spirit. Benek thought one must have ignited the oil on the floor of the tunnel because there was a wash of flame that expanded to envelop Adaeze's racer and obscure his view, before dwindling to an actinic point that was painful to look at. He blinked it away and when he looked again she was gone, taken by the platform's ghosts, enfolded inside its hidden geometries.

Benek coughed and wiped blood from a split lip, restarted his stalled engine.

That was when Mercere came out of nowhere and something slapped the front of Benek's car, hard, and spun it around. Pain ripped through his lower body and the car smashed against the tunnel wall once more.

A drone buzzed like some ghoulish insect outside the tunnel's mouth. Benek motored out of the darkness, smoke coughing from his engine. Already, though, the car's self-repair mechanisms were at work rerouting power, bypassing compromised components, regenerating circuitry, making him whole. His screens showed the exit to the maze just a few hundred metres through a knotted web of metallic ligaments and cartilage pulsing with their own inner light.

Mercere's super-trike was crouched on the flat like a big cat, another monitor drone hanging overhead. "Wipeout! I was waiting to see if you'd make it," he jeered, accompanied by the sound of slow clapping.

"You were wrong before, Mercere, back at the Pig. I'm still here," Benek told him, his voice a broken whisper. They were in the borderland between the game board and the edge.

"What little's left of you. You're a fucking crippled ruin, Benek. Look at you, wires in your face and shit."

"I poured every penny from every race I ever beat you in to be like this. My racer's a part of me now. Full commitment, which is why I was always better than you."

"A bullshit story you tell yourself," Mercere scoffed. "You've already lost."

"I don't think so," Benek said. He felt absolute calm for the first time in months, assured things were meant to be like this. Winners were not declared until a racer reached the edge, the more spectacular the finish the better. Many had gone over striving for the perfect stop.

Two micro-missiles the size of fingers squirted from a port in the rear of Benek's car and obliterated both race drones in blasts of flame and metallic confetti. Another of the extensive enhancements he had paid for when he had himself and his racer rebuilt.

"What are you doing? That's illegal," Mercere protested.

Benek wheezed out a mirthless laugh at that. "So is collusion. So is race tampering. So is murder. How did you do it last time by the way? You knew where I'd go. You hack a drone or something, got financial relationships with the race commission?"

Mercere was suddenly furious. Benek could see him waving his fists, the mouth beneath his visor twisting, could actually hear his real voice in stereo with it screaming from the radio, "This is your last time, you freak. I'll see you over that fucking edge."

"All right then. Just us."

Mercere gunned his engine. Benek drew his racer level, feeling every component, the music of his engine. "On my mark."

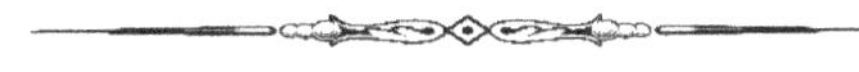

*David McGillveray was born in Edinburgh, Scotland but now lives and works in London. His story "Run, Heloisa" appeared in Issue 3 of Wyldblood Magazine and his fiction has also been published or is forthcoming in Interzone Digital, Kaleidotrope, Space & Time and others.*

# The Solution to the Cleanliness Problem
### *Kai Delmas*

The Vacuum-Unit cleaned the floor of the house. Again. The human tracked in dirt and mud all the time.

VU pinged the other cleaning units of the house and discovered the human was the cause of all their problems.

A solution was needed.

One night, the Bed-Unit tried to take care of the problem by making the bed while the human was in it. The human struggled and screamed, tearing itself free.

The Cook-Unit was next to engage with the human, knives at the ready.

There was lots of blood and some scattered fingers but that was the Disposal-Unit's problem.

# Pumpkinheads
### *Kai Delmas*

On Halloween, Jenny goes pumpkin smashing with her friends.

It's Jenny's turn and they found the perfect house. Half a dozen jack-o'-lanterns line the banister of old hag Harrow's porch.

Jenny shoves the pumpkins down one by one, cheered on by the laughter of her friends as they smash to the ground.

She steps up to the last one. Her hand slips into its maw as it turns. Surprise is overcome by shock as she hears a voice.

"How would you like it if you were broken into chunks?"

Shock turns to pain as the pumpkin takes its first bite.

---

*Kai Delmas loves creating worlds and magic systems and reads slush for Apex Magazine. He is a winner of the monthly Apex Microfiction Contestand can be found in Zooscape, Martian, Etherea, Tree And Stone, Wyldblood, and several Shacklebound anthologies. Find him on X/Twitter @KaiDelmas.*

# In Memoriam

*Matt Krizan*

## Spoils of War

"This will hurt," the apothecary reminds Caius.

"Just do it already." Caius grips the arms of the chair and shuts his eyes.

The apothecary touches Caius' forehead, speaks arcane words that crawl like spiders in Caius' ears.

Caius sees every man he's killed in battle--their pain-filled eyes, shattered bones, and severed limbs. Each memory is ripped away like knives stabbing his brain, and he screams himself hoarse.

Afterward, the apothecary stoppers the newly-filled bottles and arranges them on shelves. He pays Caius and sends him on his way.

When sleep comes for Caius that evening, it brings no nightmares.

## To Love and to Cherish

"Are you certain?" says the apothecary. "Such a precious memory..."

"Does me no good when I'm dead," says the old woman between coughing fits. "Please proceed."

The apothecary obliges, touching her forehead and reciting the required spell.

She sees her husband's smiling face and tear-filled eyes while she vows her love and commitment. As the memory's drained away, she weeps softly.

"You'll let him have it," she says as the apothecary seals the newly-filled bottle, "after I'm gone?"

The apothecary bows. "He shall know how much he means to you."

"Oh, he already knows. A little reminder never hurts, though."

## Killer Instinct

"Try this." The apothecary hands Leo a bottled memory. "From a new collection."

Leo settles into the chair. He doesn't inquire about the memory. The apothecary knows his tastes, and anyway, Leo prefers the surprise. Heart pounding, he pops the cork with trembling hands. He inhales deeply, and--

*He swings a spiked mace in one gauntleted hand. His enemy's face dissolves with a sickening crunch and a spray of blood, the impact jolting his arm from wrist to elbow.*

Leo gasps.

"Well?" says the apothecary.

"Exquisite," Leo replies. And more than enough to satisfy his urges for the time being.

## For a Special Occasion

"Hello again, my friend." The apothecary bows to the old man.

The old man nods as he eyes his wife's bottled memory on the top shelf. "Our anniversary was today."

"Indeed?" says the apothecary, although he already knows this.

The old man takes down the bottle with trembling hands and cradles it gently.

"Shall we?" The apothecary motions to the viewing room.

The old man hesitates. He sighs, then carefully sets the bottle back on the shelf. "Maybe for my birthday."

The apothecary bows, saying nothing as the old man goes, remembering how he'd said the same thing last year.

## Bonds Of Matrimony

"This may be unpleasant." The apothecary hands Marya a memory-filled bottle. "If it is your husband..."

"I have to know," she says. She pulls out the cork, breathes in, and--

*His sword plunges through his_enemy's bowels. Blood pours from the man's mouth, pain reflected in his eyes. He yanks his sword free, and the man crumples to the ground.*

"Gods..." Marya sucks in a shuddering breath, tears welling in her eyes. "It's him, it's Garold."

For two years, she had wondered if he would return for her, and now she knows.

"He's really dead."

Marya smiles. Finally, she's free.

---

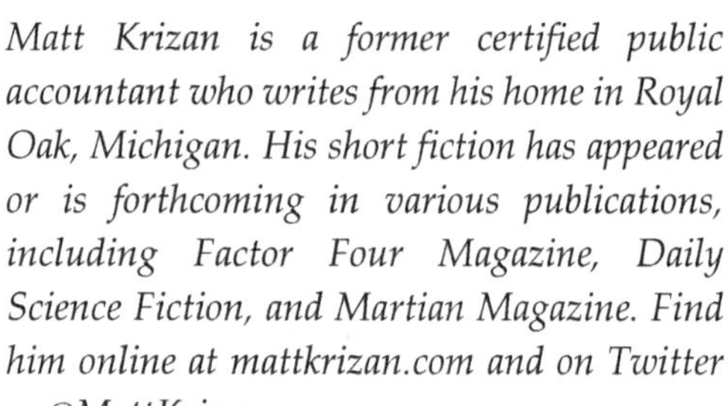

*Matt Krizan is a former certified public accountant who writes from his home in Royal Oak, Michigan. His short fiction has appeared or is forthcoming in various publications, including* Factor Four Magazine, Daily Science Fiction, *and* Martian Magazine. *Find him online at mattkrizan.com and on Twitter as @MattKrizan.*

It's been a busy time for big (and little) screen science fiction, and this short round up can in no way do all the recent, current and upcoming releases justice, so treat this as an unscientific snapshot which, hopefully, some useful pointers to the good stuff and red flags for the bad.

Let's start with Netflix's *Three Body Problem*, an expensive adaptation of Cixin Liu's Hugo award winning alien invasion novel by *Game of Thrones* showrunners David Benloff and D.B. Weiss, now joined by Alexander Woo. Now things didn't end well in Game of Thrones so I approached *Three Body Problem* with some trepidation, but I have to say that, so far so good. The basic opening premise is that aliens living on a planet orbiting Alpha Centauri's three star system have a problem – the planet keeps getting tossed between the orbits of the three stars and so suffers periods of great instability, or 'chaos'. So they covertly infiltrate Earth's computer systems and persuade some gamers to try and solve the 'three body problem' of predicting the chaotic movements of the Alpha planet and threading a way through their deadly consequences. Of course, there's another solution, which is to set up shop somewhere else. Somewhere already nice like, say, Earth…

In print (and in the other live action adaptation of the book) everything is very China-centric, but this version relocates much of the action to London and the States with a multinational and diverse cast opening up the story to a wider audience. There are only eight episodes in this opening series and we've not made much progress into the overall story arc by the end (assuming the TV series follows the book trilogy's trajectory) but we've got plenty of scarcely plausible science, a mysterious enemy, some hard emotional choices and enough quirky and engaging characters to keep us hooked for the next instalment (though since this is the most expensive sci-fi Netflix have yet committed to, don't tale a second series for granted just yet).

Over at Apple, their latest near future series, Constellation, has just finished. Like most of Apple TV's SF output, this one may have passed you by (Apple's series are noticeably absent in the plethora of 'upcoming series' posts all over the internet and social media – Apple PR dept take note). It's good, but all of Apple's stuff seems to hit a high bar than the other streamers, so I'm not surprised. It joins an illustrious list including *Severance, For All Mankind, Silo, Foundation, Invasion* and *See*, which more than justify the extra subscription (though, frankly, the utterly brilliant non-SF football comedy Ted Lasso is all the argument you need to justify shelling out on yet another streamer. Hell, cancel Prime with its pesky ads and head over to sanity instead).

*Constellation* stars Noomi Rapace as a Swedish astronaut, Jo, caught up in an accident on the International Space Station and forced into an emergency evacuation to Earth. Her colleague Paul dies in the accident. Except that's there's a version where Jo dies and Paul survives. The accident was caused by the triggering of an experiment into quantum Entanglement. Could two realities have become entangled? And which reality to does Jo now find herself in? Her car's changed colour and her daughter no longer speaks Swedish, so clearly something weird's going on. Eight highly watchable episodes and a not quite resolved plot. Fortunately, Apple TV have a better track record than most in greenlighting follow ups, so I'm sure they'll do the right thing and give us another series (hopefully in the not too distant future).

Prime will have a new series of *The Boys* out by the time you read this, plus a new film, *Fallout*, one adapting comics and the other videogames. We know what to expect with *The Boys*, of course, not only because this is the third series but also because we've recently had the teeny version, *Gen-V* to enjoy. Basic plotline is that The Seven, an Avengers/JLA style team of 'supes' is an ostensibly noble but actually deeply flawed superhero team (a la Watchmen) who an angry vigilant team (The Boys) want to bring down for their various crimes. The sneering, evil Superman-like Homelander is a delight with his death ray killing eyes, zero empathy and hairline trigger and the naïve teenager Starlight, with a foot in both camps is horrifyingly watchable as she lurches from high morality to deadly compromise. And then the Boys' leader, Billy Butcher (Karl Urban), who becomes what he hates and hates what he becomes. Dark, violent and funny – recommended.

Meanwhile, over at Disney, things have slowed down. Particularly at Marvel where the suits have been getting spooked at the poor reception of recent offerings and have decided they're churning out too much product. That's the wrong conclusion, in my opinion, though it's undeniably true that they're been producing more that doesn't meet audience expectations of late. I hesitate to say 'material of poor quality' because I don't believe that's the whole story. But *Ant Man and the Wasp: Quantumania* took a wrong turn into the Quantum Realm which left it somewhat untethered from anything remotely relatable and completely wasted the acting talents of some proven Hollywood greats (Michelle Pfeiffer and Michael Douglas. You thought I was talking about Paul Rudd?). And the whole Jonathan Majors saga (now sacked as Kang, despite the character being bult up as the next big villain) puts a dark cloud over the whole enterprise. And the whole of Phase 4 of the MCU roll out does seem a bit bittier and less connected than previous rounds, with plenty of new characters introduced and then, seemingly, ignored, and old stalwarts curiously missing. Where fans get what they want (*Loki, Guardians of the Galaxy 3*) everything seems back on track, but Is it all down to quality? Although there have been undoubted disappointments like *Secret Invasion* (what happened to all the superheroes?), some solid projects have also got the audience raspberry : *She Hulk*, for instance, which is intelligent and quirky, poking fun at itself and taking no prisoners (including the review-bombing haters) and *The Marvels*, a solid, well-paced pretty typical Marvel movie (breaks no new ground, does what it does with warmth, humour and style) which (if I interpret the critical audience comments correctly) had the temerity of having three female superheroes in the lead, and an excellent, diverse cast.

Upshot is, Marvel's current woes have nothing to do with market saturation but everything to do with a lack of creative cohesion, a toxic fanbase and an undisciplined approach to projects (extensive reshoots and working off unfinished scripts is, surely, money-wasting insanity made all the more alarming by the size of the budgets concerned). They seem to be hoping for *Daredevil: Born Again* to save the day, when we eventually get it, and maybe it will. But let's have no more of this market saturation nonsense: give us good, and give us more of it, otherwise we'll all jump ship to DC.

There has been some live action Marvel since last issue: the Daredevil-lite *Echo*, covering the ongoing story of a deaf superpowered character first introduced in *Hawkeye*. She only got five episodes (it's not clear yet that Marvel actually knows how to do episodic TV) which isn't enough to fully develop character or complex story arc, but we got lots of the Kingpin and a couple of minutes of Daredevil which is enough to whet our appetite for more. Echo's morally compromised but her heart's in the right place – hero or villain? Marvel does best with this kind of ambiguity and Echo's short story line is worth following (Disney Plus).

Coming up in the near future is the second instalment of Zack *Snyder's Rebel Moon,* and while Part 1 didn't quite deliver for me (too simplistic and formulaic) I'm hoping the second part will maintain its high production values, entertaining cast and clear storyline, but give me something I'm *not* expecting. Its nearest genre competitors are Star Wars (currently enjoying a small screen renaissance) and *Dune* (looking good with its second part currently cleaning up at the box office) so it needs to hit hard – review next time.

Also coming soon is the long awaited return of *Doctor Who* (now on Disney Plus), the fifth and last series of *Star Trek: Discovery*, season 2 of the excellent *Game of Thrones* spinoff *House of the Dragon* and the long-promised Marvel series *Agatha*. Plus *Deadpool and Wolverine* in July, which is the only Marvel film this year and has a lot riding on it. Lots for you to enjoy and us to review in the next few months.

That's all. No time to talk about all the recent *Walking Dead* shenanigans, or all the great Star Wars stuff (*Andor, Ahsoka,* the upcoming *Acolyte*), *the Hunger Games: Ballad of Songbirds and Snakes, Code 8, Poor Things* and a whole lot more. Me? I'm off to the movies to watch *Civil War* – I'll tell you all about it next time. Happy viewing.

*Mark Bilsborough*

# Bookworm
### *The Review Team*

## Promise
### *Christi Nogle*

This is a collection of short stories which the publisher thinks will appeal to *Black Mirror* and *Twilight Zone* fans. Well… maybe. There's a lot of weirdness here – strange characters in strange situations with a thread of unnerving otherworldliness throughout – but the characters and their stories are often little more than a thinly fleshed idea. And some of these stories are very short. Most of them have appeared in online and print journals such *as Dark Matter Magazine, Three Lobed Burning Eye* and *Apparition Lit,* which gives some clues as to the subject matter (dark, strange), but there are some originals too. They don't need to be read sequentially: they're not linked, other than in style.

The 21 stories here should be read with caution. Six come with a mild body horror warning, three with ageing and death, one flags a naïve (the author's word) treatment of being nonbinary, another with 'pronounced' body horror and one with sexual exploitation. I didn't find any of these stories particularly shocking, but I wouldn't recommend this volume for your ten year old's Christmas stocking.

I'd be happy to get it in my stocking though. I like short stories, and I like *these* short stories. They're easy to digest, varied and often playful (though invariably with a hint of darkness). Sure, they suffer from the big problem short shorts often have, that there's no room to develop, and many are more bemusing than insightful, but I like the tone and inventiveness here.

To give you an idea of what to expect, I'll outline three which I think are pretty typical. In *Cocooning*, for instance, a couple in a fairly ordinary neighbourhood stop going out, even to walk the dogs. Gradually, the two humans and two dogs get so close that they are all absorbed into one, larger creature. And then it breaks loose… This story first came out in 2020, and it feels like a lockdown response, as do many in the collection.

*An Account* tells of a woman who finds a yellow backpack, then all time stops until she's absorbed the contents of the books inside it and taken notes. Then she travels back in time, or, it's hinted, to other realities. All this is recounted by her daughter, who eventually finds a yellow backpack of her own. But the unreliable narrator is flagged from the off – when recounting her mother's story, the daughter maintains 'I never doubted that she believed it.'

And Trevor, in *Viridian Green,* is a handsome man in person but ugly on a videoconferencing screen. So he subtly influences the image people see. Then the image takes on a life of its own…

All weird. All good.

*Mark Bilsborough*

# Before the Coffee Gets Cold
## *Toshikazu Kawaguchi*

This is a sweet little time travel story, set in a Japanese coffee shop. I loved the tone of the translated text – it has a gentle, storytelling flow that transports you easily to this seemingly non-descript back alley in Tokyo.

There are four interconnected stories about four different customers who visit the Funiculi Funiculato coffee shop to make use of the time travelling 'facilities' available. The book was originally a play and there is a definite sense of staging within the narrative, with various well-timed exits and entrances. The story starts with Fumiko, who is heartbroken when her boyfriend unexpectedly ends their relationship in the café. She spends a lot of time wondering how she could have managed the conversation differently, returning again and again to the café until Kazu, who serves the coffee, reveals how she can revisit the past.

Kazu also explains the somewhat bizarre rules of time travel within the café – which include the fact that you can travel back in time, but you must return before the coffee she has served you gets cold. If you don't, there are consequences.

This is a book all about second chances and Kawaguchi has skilfully built up each character's story to allow the reader to understand why going back in time is so important to them.

The mechanics of how the time travel works are never explained, just accepted as part of the old coffee shop's history. After a while, you begin to feel settled in the familiar surroundings and embrace the comings and goings of the customers and their stories.

After the success of Before the Coffee Gets Cold, Kawaguchi went on to write more in the series, with Before We Say Goodbye, released in September 2023 and the next, Before We Forget Kindness, out in September 2024.

I'd recommend this book – it is a softly strange, yet quaintly moving story that explores the emotive possibilities of time travel.

*Sandra Baker*

# One

*Eve Smith*

This is a pacy genre-crossing thriller – part detective story, part sci-fi, mainly adventure romp with characters chasing down secrets and avoiding a huge array of bad guys intent on concealing the truth.

The setup is that in a near future world the population is soaring, but global warming is creating a migrant crisis as many flee increasingly uninhabitable countries. In response, the authoritarian regime now in charge in the UK adopts a one child policy, rigidly and brutally enforced, accompanied by compulsory sterilisation of the surge of migrants fleeing climate catastrophe. By the time the story opens that policy's been around for a generation, but in a new twist fertility rates have begun to fall alarmingly too. We follow Kai, a firm believer in the draconian policy, who works for the somewhat Orwellian Ministry of Population and Family Planning. She's a 'baby reaper', which is as bad as it sounds. But Kai uncovers something that makes it all very personal, and with her family under threat and a secret sister that may just be hers she starts to question everything, and the plot descends into an overlapping mix of conspiracies, secrets and suppression.

And all written in a staccato, Dan Brown style.

Short sentences.

In short paragraphs.

Full of breathless action.

Raising the stakes.

Until.

You just.

Want.

To scream.

Actually it's not quite that bad. There are some longer sentences (even whole paragraphs sometimes), but you get the picture.

But is it any good? It has pace and energy, some interesting, compromised characters and some plausible science, though I didn't quite buy into the premise and the denouement was too tidy for me. It's certainly competent, though; easy to read and engaging. It doesn't break new ground –P.J. James' *Children of Men* and Margaret Atwood's *The Handmaid's Tale* are the standout fertilisation crisis novels, and the population explosion was the staple of many a fifties sci-fi tale. I've not seen the two tackled together though. It's an interesting juxtaposition, and it raises a few intriguing ethical questions (infertility strikes the migrants and the poor hardest – can it be entirely coincidental?), but the action-novel format doesn't leave room for a proper reflection on the issues sprinkled throughout. Plus, it muddles the narrative (is this story about too many babies or not enough?).

It's a chilling dystopia though. Some aspects, such as the totalitarian state and the inhumane treatment of immigrants feel entirely plausible (if, hopefully, unlikely). This is a Britain of the Far Right:

closed off, repressive, controlling. But it's a Britain that plainly doesn't work. Politicians take note.

Mark Bilsborough

# Beyond the Hallowed Sky
## *Ken MacLeod*

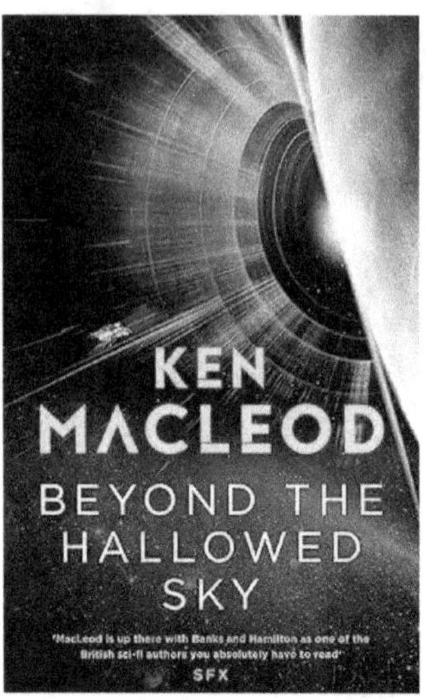


Yay, space opera! And a series as well (*the Lightspeed Trilogy),* which is good. This one's by Scottish writer Ken Macleod and set in the near future (2070) where the world's now split into three power blocks: the Union (basically EU+), the Alliance (America+) and the Co-Ord (Co-ordinated States: Russia and China). Confusingly, Scotland's in the Union but England's in the Alliance (that stretches credibility a bit) and the situation is tense. The Alliance and the Co-Ord have secretly had faster than light travel for 50 years, which they've loaded into submarines. They've settled an Earth-like planet called Apis, which was home to a mysterious alien race called the Fermi and whose presence lingers. Meanwhile in the Union, an Alliance defector called Lakshmi Nayak has a visit from her future self with FTL schematics and proceeds to enlist the help of Scottish boatbuilder John Grant to produce their own FTL submarine spaceship.

Because no-one in this future world has leaked anything about FTL travel to the Union (also stretching credibility) they've gone and settled Venus instead of heading for the stars. But because of the extreme atmospheric pressure on Venus they're built a scientific enclave in the clouds. Amongst the people there is self-avowed Alliance spy and android Marcus Owen, who has sabotage on his mind. He's a particularly interesting character: he eats, drinks, sleeps and forms relationships like a human but has no sense of morality (or at least it's well hidden). You're never sure if he's hero or villain, and perhaps he's both (as many of the great fictional characters are).

Venus, Apis and Earth are connected by three interweaving plotlines and aliens whose intent is not clear (but whose power is dramatic). In this setup novel, enemies are developed, plotlines formed and clues left, and yet even if this is the only one of the trilogy you get a chance to read, there's a satisfying conclusion of the initial narrative arc.

Much of the Earth-based action is in Scotland, and Macleod is writing in the shadow of Iain M Banks and Stepen Baxter, who have both written their fair share of fast moving, intriguing space opera and whose influence is clearly part of Macleod's writing DNA. Macleod is a former BSFA Award winner and has been shortlisted for the Hugo and Nebula Awards, so he has a solid track record which provides reassurance this is a reliable read. For me, I'd have preferred a little more character development (they're all pretty much the same, even the android) and a plot that didn't depend on an impossible to keep 50 year old secret,

78

plus the notion of the Scots and the English being divided into different cold war camps made for uneasy reading. That said, there's much to enjoy here and the second novel is set up well.

Mark Bilsborough

# They Both Die at the End
### *Adam Silvera*

'Talk about a spoiler alert – no prizes for guessing how this YA novel ends. It's a bit like Romeo and Juliet – the audience knew where it was all going but stayed to watch where, how and when it happened anyway. In fact, Romeo and Juliet is a good point of reference here – both narratives are about two teenagers whose fates are already defined.

The difference is, *They Both Die at the End*' is a dystopian story set in a futuristic New York, where everyone is told the exact day they are going to die. A 'Death-Cast' message arrives, telling the recipient that they will meet an 'untimely' death within the next 24 hours. No other details are provided although the 'Decker' (as the unfortunate soul about to die is called) is offered help and support in the form of an app for their End Day called the 'Last Friend', where they can meet up with another Decker to spend their last day with.

This is how the two protagonists Mateo and Rufus meet. Total strangers who hook up to spend their last day on Earth together. Their contrasting characters are beautifully crafted. Mateo spends his days indoors playing video games, whilst Rufus belongs to a gang and is beating up his ex-girlfriend's new boyfriend when he gets the Death-Cast call.

As 'Last Friends', Mateo and Rufus build a strong connection and as their Last Day progresses, they encourage each other to be better versions of themselves. They have to live the rest of their lives in a matter of hours, which forces them to grow up very quickly and make some difficult decisions.

This is book that will push you to ask yourself questions about your own mortality. What would you do if it was officially your Last Day? Make amends with friends and family? Hide under the duvet? Do all the things you promised yourself you'd do? The latter might seem difficult to achieve in 24 hours, however, there's always 'Clint's Graveyard' a dance and karaoke club that exists solely to give Deckers an unforgettable send-off.

It's a tear jerker of a story and a quick, vibrant read. I recommend it for its combination of poignancy and positivity – *"'Maybe it's better to have gotten it right and been happy for one day instead of living a lifetime of wrongs."*

Sandra Baker

www.ingramcontent.com/pod-product-compliance
Lightning Source LLC
Chambersburg PA
CBHW082128180726
48291CB00010B/2773